THE SPINNING WHEEL

THE GRIMM STAR SAGA: FIRST LIGHT BOOK 1

J. DARLENE EVERLY

J. DARLENE EVERLY

THE SPINNING WHEEL

The Grimm Star Saga: First Light Book 1

Hardcover: ISBN 978-1-954719-05-7

Paperback: ISBN 978-1-954719-04-0

Ebook: ISBN 978-2-954719-03-3

First paperback edition February 2021

Edited by Beth Hale, Magnolia Editing

Cover design by Jupiter Alley

Formatted by Beth Hale, Magnolia Editing

✿ Created with Vellum

The Spinning Wheel is just the beginning of The Grimm Star Saga: First Light, if you would like to be the first to know about the next book in the series, get a free book in The Grimm Star Universe, and learn about the other books the author has written, please go to jdarleneeverly.com and sign up for her newsletter.

DEDICATION

This book is dedicated to my hero, my Grandpa, I wish he was
here to hold it in his hands.

ZELLENDINE

Zellendine stared into the dark void of space, as the first tendrils of light from the sun the ship approached started to come into view, while she tried to pretend what she was about to do was something she wanted.

"Don't forget to bring a holo with you," her father, Stephen, said as he walked through the clinic behind her.

She didn't turn around. She knew what she needed to bring, and she would follow all the protocols she had been taught. In no galaxy, this one or the last, would she let her father know how much she didn't want to be a part of a birthing.

The sun coming into view would be theirs in their new home on the planet the dilapidated ship was heading to. They weren't really getting close to the large sun; there would be two planetary orbits between them and the Grimm star, as they called it, on the ship's track to their new home planet. But the dark, familiar view out the windows would soon be completely filled with light as the Wheel, their ship, made its way past.

For now, it remained mostly dark, and she thought about

how rare it was that the children they waited on would be born right before the ship's dawn.

"Come on," Stephen said, coming in behind her again. He gave a heavy sigh and his hand touched her shoulder.

Zellendine turned to look back at him, forcing a bland smile onto her face.

"Do you need me to take care of both births today, or should I go over everything with you again?" he asked. His dark eyes were soft and reminded her of the early days of her childhood when he still read her bedtime stories from the holo.

"No, Dad- sorry, Stephen. I'm fine. I was just checking out our new star," she said, stepping out from under his hand and picking up the holo on the table next to the door.

Stephen stepped up to the window and looked toward the edges of the solar flares. The window automatically filtered the rays so they could see it clearly, and it had been a while since they were near enough to a star to see the light show they produced. It surprised her he hadn't noticed before.

"Our star, our sun." His voice was low and reverent. "I hope its light is good to us."

"What do you mean?" Zellendine asked. Even though her voice was quiet, it sounded loud in her ears, she wasn't expecting to speak her question out loud.

"Have you heard anything? I mean, from Briar last shift?" He didn't answer her question, but at least she thought she had a better idea of what he was getting at.

"No. He doesn't usually say much about the terraforming department." He nodded as she spoke, and she drew her brows together over her own dark eyes that looked so much like his.

"Don't you know anyone in terraforming you could ask your questions to?" she asked, he was part of leadership and he was friends with people he could have gone to, so why was he bothering to try and get information via her friend?

Stephen made a hmm noise and shook his head again, still avoiding telling her anything that would actually help her to understand what his words meant.

Zellendine rubbed along her jaw and tried not to grind her teeth. Her father and his talking in circles made her want to shake him sometimes.

"It doesn't matter. I'm sure we'll find our way," he said, turning from the window and walking out, not bothering to wait to see if she was coming after him. No one ever bothered to question if she would follow when it was required of her.

With no choice but to trail along, she turned and did just that.

Maybe, she thought, once they reached their new planet, she would be able to stop walking in her father's footsteps.

But they were still one hundred years in stasis, the rest of this shift, and another month after waking, away from that arrival and any possibilities it held.

"Just so you're prepared," Stephen said, as they exited the clinic and headed down the hall to the birthing room, "chances are, there will be a lot of people there."

"I thought that only happened last shift because the baby was born to a member of the leadership council," she said. Sweat broke out at the nape of her neck and her heart thumped painfully in her chest the second the words were out of his mouth. She gripped the holo tighter lest her hands started to shake too.

"No, birth days are almost always a party atmosphere." His voice was jovial, like he thought it was fine to have more than just the families present.

She couldn't imagine a more private occasion than the first moments someone met a new family member, to say nothing of the fact that it meant a huge audience for her biggest challenge as a medic yet.

Zellendine took a deep breath and reminded herself that nothing ever went wrong with the births. The computers, taking their cues from the far off first Chapter programming, always ensured everything went fine. It didn't matter that she was still an apprentice medic, or that this was her first solo delivery; everything would be just fine.

But no matter the repeated words in her head, her hands grew clammy and the small of her back started to sweat too.

2

TROYLUS

HE STOPPED IN THE HALLWAY SO A GROUP OF PEOPLE COULD hurry past him. The hoards of people headed to the birthing room were giving him a headache and he wasn't even in there with them yet. Damn crowd couldn't just let people have babies without pushing their way into the day.

Troylus tried to take a deep breath through his nose and blow it out of his mouth; he tried to calm the anger coursing through his veins. Somehow, he had to get through this, to get to the birthing room and talk to Zellendine without lashing out again.

Of all the symptoms of whatever was wrong with him, the absolutely untethered rage he felt even planning to be around Zellendine was the worst part.

Sure, he wanted his eye back to normal, and he was worried that it seemed to be spreading, but the anger at his friend, for no real reason he could make sense of, was making him pissed off at everything in general which didn't make it easier to stop being mad at her.

"Hey, Troylus," one of the members of the engineering crew said as he passed him in the hall, a big goofy grin on his face.

Troylus merely nodded in return.

It was hard enough to keep his concentration on tamping down his anger, keeping himself in check, without the random interruption of people he couldn't take the time to deal with.

At least, he couldn't afford the time right at that moment.

The floor lurched below him with a rumble from the engine room that reverberated through the entire ship. It was acting up a lot this shift.

He had woken up irrationally pissed off at one of his oldest friends, with the engines showing their age more than he could remember them ever doing before, and now his eye was slowly turning from green to silver.

Officially, he hated this shift.

By the time he reached his destination, the strangely sterile room was full of people milling about, and Zellendine was already there, tapping away at a holo and occasionally glancing up from what she was doing to look at the mechanical womb in front of her.

In another time, another shift, he would have gone to her side with a smile and an encouraging word, but at that moment he had to swallow down a nasty comment. A nasty comment about her, targeting her for no reason other than that she was there with her long blonde hair trailing down her back and her dark eyes intent on her job.

Deep breath, he reminded himself. This was Zellendine. He knew her. They had been friends for as long as he could remember. It was him, Briar, and Zellendine in their little corner of the ship, the same age and the same shift, working together to grow up among the hallways and the computers and the stars, perpetually heading forward and pretending to forget the past. But it was the past he was looking to for help now. No matter that it was against the law. He needed it. He thought about Zellendine of the past, the girl who helped him climb the trees in the orchard in the years she was taller than he was and he needed a boost. If he could hold that Zellendine in his mind while he talked to her, maybe he could keep his wrath in check. And he better. He needed her help.

3

ZELLENDINE

"My baby," Yanna said, tenderly caressing the metal lid of the mechanical womb as if it was the child itself.

"Our baby," Anders said, on the other side of the machine, doing the same with a smile on his face. They reached across the lid to each other, holding hands.

A screen mounted on the side of the womb showed everyone the healthy vital signs of the tiny being inside.

The women whose baby was in the other tank, were doing the same across the room. They had only recently been informed from the final DNA scan which egg was used and they would never know which sperm sample was used; the computer chose all of that and kept it in files no one could access.

Zellendine was never comfortable in this small space with its four wombs. It was one of the only places on the ship that didn't have a patch on some surface or another. There weren't worn tracks on wood floors, instead it had sleek white metal floors that rang in a tinny, hollow way with each step someone took. Which meant that with the crowds, the sound of steps created a discordant music. The place looked as pristine as it must have the day the ship took off from their last colonized planet, before she was even born. All the surfaces were bright white instead of the dark and stained ones she was used to in the rest of the ship.

Besides, the birth itself always seemed too intimate, too much a family only experience. After all, only the immediate family of the infant stayed awake for the first year of the baby's life to bond, changing shifts entirely in the process.

She rolled her head around on her neck and tried to focus on her job. The Chapter computers knew what was best, she reminded herself. Who was she to question the wisdom of the Chapter computers? They had placed her here. She had to trust that and focus on moving forward. That was the mission, and she would follow it, burying her illegal doubt and never ever giving it free rein over her thoughts, let alone her actions.

Zellendine's dad was attending across the room for the other couple. He was matched by the computer to them for the initial screening and cleaning of their child.

The room was thick with onlookers she tried her best to ignore, even some of the starwalkers, the people who went outside the ship for repairs, were milling around.

Birthdays were supposed to be a party, she reminded herself. The ultimate manifestation of always moving forward, the ship philosophy.

"Zellendine," Troylus said, tugging on her elbow. His messy light brown hair hung in his face and she wanted to remind him that the rules stated he needed to keep it back. But Troylus never listened to her.

"Troylus," Zellendine said, pulling her arm from his grasp. She had a job to do here, she was the medic on duty for Anders and Yanna's baby, damn it. What was he doing? "You should mingle, but you shouldn't be talking to me."

He sneered at her and shook his head before he spun on his

heel. His stomping footfalls as he marched away managed to be loud enough that Zellendine heard them over the conversations around her. She felt bad that she was rude and took a step after him, but whatever Troylus wanted would have to wait, because the womb in front of her started to rattle. The sound of the internal mechanisms leaping into action made her hands shake, and a small amount of the fluid inside trickled out of the soft opening in the bottom that bulged as the baby was pushed toward it.

This was the kind of thing she was trained for, this was what the computer said she was meant to do. She just had to move forward and trust it was right.

Yanna and Anders both made excited sounds and bent to watch.

An echoing cry went up across the room as the same process started there. The conversations around them ebbed away.

Zellendine set her holo aside and bent into position below the womb, waiting for the baby she was in charge of attending to make its appearance. It was only the second birth she had attended. But this time, it was all on her.

She glanced around and couldn't find Troylus among the crowd. He had wanted to apprentice as a medic but was instead a starwalker with his father, which was what Zellendine had always wanted to be. Whatever metric the first Chapter founders had used in their computer systems were a mystery. People rarely got the assignment they wanted, but all of them kept moving forward.

Which meant that instead of keeping the outside of the ship repaired and prepping for the building of all they would need once they reached the planet, Zellendine was bent below a bulging mechanical womb, her hands growing wet with the fluid dripping from it, reaching up to catch the baby as it was expelled, in all its slime covered glory.

The baby was so small; she knew it would be, but the fragility of the baby's size still struck her and made her movements gentler in an instant. It had a tiny fuzzing of reddish hair in a small patch on the top of its head.

Wiping the baby down and turning it over to look in its eyes, she froze.

"Dad," Zellendine yelled, the cheers from the room stopped, everyone shocked she had called him by the intimate title outside the confines of their living quarters, but she couldn't think about her mistake. Not when a dead child was in her hands. Her father ran to her side, himself coated in the fluid from the baby he had just caught.

"It didn't make it," she whispered into her father's ear as he bent his head down for a closer examination of the infant who looked whole, but wasn't breathing, and had no heartbeat.

He went to work on the child, trying to get life to come back to the tiny corpse, barking orders at Zellendine that she followed without question. But their work amounted to nothing. The spark was gone.

Anders and Yanna wept and cried out, grasping at each other and begging her and her dad to do something, inconsolable in their grief. The people that had gathered for a joyous occasion drifted out of the room. And Zellendine finished cleaning up the tiny body, wrapping it in a little green blanket, while the living baby across the room cried.

4

TROYLUS

ZELLENDINE PISSED HIM OFF. WELL, A LOT OF PEOPLE PISSED HIM off, but Zellendine had the ability to piss Troylus off worse than almost anyone else he knew on the ship. That wasn't just the new rage. Her unique skill had started years ago.

When they were kids, she was his first friend, then Briar's little sister was born, and he transferred to their shift. After that they were a team and the other people around their age on their shift never penetrated into their tight knot of friendship.

Somewhere along the line she grew more trusting of the Chapter and their computers, living with a singular devotion to the ship law to always move forward and he... had not. He wanted to shake her, to force her to see that they were all having their choices taken from them by a computer that was notoriously wrong.

It was filled with tech from before their ship took off from their last planet, but no one was allowed to even look at what the programming was if they wanted to focus on what was ahead of them, so it just continued to get more and more outdated.

Briar would understand, when he woke up. Briar would find a way to get Zellendine to look at Troylus's eye and help him. Troylus just had to wait that long. He told himself to be patient over and over, but his steps along the old planks of the corridor were heavier because she hadn't noticed, and he wasn't sure he could stand to wait much longer.

If his eye continued to change, he was going to have to say something. She was the medic, she was supposed to help. He didn't want to go to Stephen, her father. Stephen was part of the leadership team. There might be something irreversibly wrong with him and Troylus thought, in his less charitable moments, that he couldn't trust leadership not to punish him for whatever the hell was happening to him.

Passing through to the small starwalking office off the air lock, he breathed in the familiar smells of the room that made his nose itch. Visiting Briar in the terraforming office smelled of soil samples, the terrarium bay with the orchard smelled the way he imagined nature did, but in here, the general scent of the ship, decay and worn down overheated metal, was stronger than almost anywhere else. His favorite smell on the ship was the medic office. That place always smelled of clean bandages and antiseptic, it was no small part of the reason he wished he could work there.

At least I'm not in engineering, he thought, as he took his seat and stared out the curved window toward the growing tendrils of solar flares.

"How did the birth go?" Rullon, his father, asked, leaning back in his chair and rubbing his hands over his face. His jowls hung, more pronounced at the end of the day, but he tried to smile.

"I don't know. It was too packed in there, so I left, but the machines were making noise. How's the team outside?" Troylus asked, trying to smile back.

"Ah, they're fine. Just regular check on the center rotation joint." Rullon waved his hand in a dismissive gesture and his face went back to far away and smiling. "Those mech wombs are amazing." He bent back to the chart of comets and asteroids on his holo.

"Yeah." Troylus bent his head to his own holo, pretending to work on his own task, checking the dwindling supply of things they could use to patch the outside. But they all knew they didn't have much left, and if they had too much trouble before they reached the planet they would have to start dismantling more things inside the ship. Instead, he stared at the program Briar gave him the last time they had been together. It was full of charts on oxygen and other gas calculations from the probes sent to the planet so many thousands of years ago, and the estimates of what might be happening on the planet now. He didn't want to think about the wombs, about the babies being born. He had started in the same mechanical womb as those children, and they would live under the same rules he did, but by the time they could remember anything about their lives, they would all be on the planet.

He had imagined what it would be like, to place his feet on a planet, to feel nature, not the false version they cultivated in the terrarium on the ship with all the plants kept small and contained and the animals carefully managed. He had imagined what the word wild meant, but it made him nervous. He wanted it. He wanted the possibilities of it, the choice present in it, but it didn't exist in his life, and he wasn't sure what all it meant.

And none of his thoughts, the ones about the ship, the computer, the Chapters, or his friends, were things he could share. Not if he wanted to see the planet. And he did. Desperately.

"Rullon, with these estimates, how long do you think it will take for us to terraform?" he asked, tilting his holo and the graph toward his dad. His dad was vaguely interested in what the terraforming department thought they would encounter once they landed, only because the starwalkers were supposed to be the first people to step foot on the planet and build what everyone else needed.

"It isn't the gases I'm worried about. If the estimates run true, then we will probably be able to breathe right away." Rullon turned back to his own holo and chewed on a fingernail.

"What is it?" Troylus asked, fighting the urge to chew on his own fingernails.

"The biggest question I have is, how stable is the environment? If it's not stable enough it could be deadly and we could have problems growing anything, let alone enough to feed everyone. If it's too stable, how much life is on the planet?" Rullon said, his voice hushed and his fingernail back between his teeth.

"Life. You don't mean life like us?" Troylus asked, the thought never having crossed his mind.

"Not like us exactly, no. But enough like us that we would need to find another planet."

His dad's words were like a small chip in a window in Troylus's mind. The lines of them, the possibilities, spidering out faster than the ship was hurtling through space. Troylus didn't want to think about it. He didn't want to think about the slim chance they had that they would find a planet in the perfect moment for their arrival.

Troylus wanted off the ship, if the planet was already home to animals like them… his heart sped up and his stomach landed somewhere in his feet.

5

ZELLENDINE

Anders and Yanna were left to spend a day with their baby, to say goodbye to the hopes they had for the tiny bundle in their arms. Stephen said it was the only way they would be able to keep moving forward.

Zellendine spent the day tearing apart the mechanical womb with Mohammed, a member of the robotics team, trying to find a malfunction.

"This doesn't make any sense," he muttered, staring at a holoscreen connected to the womb by a cord with a plug in that looked like a tangle of gelatinous wires.

"What doesn't?" she said, putting back together the fluid pump using new tubes.

"I expected a malfunction, but there isn't any. There isn't even any reading that the baby died. It was alive one minute and being born, and then it was born and dead the next minute." His fingers were flying through the commands and lists of information on the holo that didn't mean anything to Zellendine.

"But there has to be something wrong with the machine,

right?" she asked, already understanding that this riddle wasn't going to have an easy answer.

"No, damn it. There's nothing here..." His voice trailed off and he stared into the middle distance between himself and the wall.

Zellendine stopped what she was doing, trying to understand what was weighing on this man so heavily, like he was in a heightened gravity space altogether.

He looked up and shook his head. "My partner and I were planning on having a baby during the approach, delaying our landing, but now..."

It was exactly what she was worried about. How many people wouldn't even take the risk if they knew about the death? Who would put themselves through that for a year before they finally stepped foot on their new planet?

She reached out and placed her finger on the knuckle of his pinkie, not willing to fully cross the line and place her hand over his, but wanting to offer some support. It was all she could do. She didn't have any wisdom to offer him on his decision. Especially since Mohammed's partner could have a hard time with dysphoria if he was forced by circumstance to stop his medication in order to try and give birth himself once they were on the planet. No matter the risk, the questionable womb might have remained their best option.

Over the communication port by the door, the sound of static preceded an announcement for all members of the leadership team to make their way to the gathering room.

Zellendine brushed off her hands and raised her brows to Mohammed. He nodded at her, letting her know it was okay to leave him there to finish the process of putting the womb back together.

She wasn't a member of leadership, no apprentices were, but

her dad had told her they would want an update on the machine and probably an account from her since she was the attendant.

Outside the door to the gathering room, Troylus was waiting for her, pushing through the group of leadership members making their way inside.

Trying not to have any of these people, who held sway over so much of what happened on the ship, know that Troylus's rudeness had anything to do with her, Zellendine pulled back and tucked herself around the corner.

Her fists clenched at her sides as she ground her teeth, waiting for him to get to her.

Troylus stormed around the corner and Zellendine rounded on him.

"What do you think you're doing?" she asked.

"I need to talk to you," Troylus yelled.

She waved her hands in the air and held her finger to her lips. Outside a meeting of the leadership team was the last place for him to yell and break decorum. Not to mention, if she swore at him, which was likely, then she could be punished too.

"Fine. Then talk, but you have sixty seconds," Zellendine said, trying and failing to keep the snarl out of her voice.

"There's something wrong with my eye," Troylus said, his voice tremulous as he pushed his hair out of his face and pointed at his right eye.

"Oh, for fuck's sake, Troylus. Damn it. Now I'm swearing. If you're having trouble with your vision, then come to the clinic later. Right now, I have to talk to leadership." She made to walk past him, fuming that he would try and delay her for something so small.

"I'm not having trouble with my vision, but this is important." Troylus shoved his hand out to block Zellendine from going around the corner.

"Stop it." Zellendine swatted his hand away. "This isn't about you, right now. A baby is dead."

Troylus slammed his mouth shut and ground his jaw. Zellendine realized she had been too harsh. But the baby's death was important, and she was scared it suggested something larger than she was able to understand. She had never heard of anything like it ever happening on board the Wheel.

She grabbed at Troylus's retreating back, catching his sleeve, and he yanked his arm out of her grasp.

"Go. Have your moment in front of the leadership. Suck up like you always do. I'm sure Briar will be so proud of you when he wakes up," Troylus said, stomping off down the hallway, his heavy steps ricocheting off the patched metal walls in a discordant pattern.

What the hell was wrong with him now? And why would Briar care about one more argument between her and Troylus? She asked a million questions in her mind, trying and failing to figure him out.

Zellendine shook her head, straightened her jacket and headed into the gathering room. She and Troylus had been arguing about things large and small since before they received their apprenticeships, but this shift was the first time she thought he truly didn't like her. There was nothing she could do about it except wait until Troylus had worked through his anger and always move forward, a lesson she wished he would learn.

6

TROYLUS

TROYLUS CLENCHED HIS FISTS AT HIS SIDES AND GROUND HIS teeth. Damn it, but Zellendine just *refused* to help him. Again. She hadn't seen it. How? It was taking over his eye.

He rubbed his eye with a thumb; just thinking about it made it itch. What the hell was happening to him?

The hallway in front of him seemed to sway and he knew he couldn't go back to the office. If he tried, he was likely to screw up and blurt out something to his dad. Rullon didn't need to get dragged into this.

Rullon had asked him that morning when he was going to cut his hair, or at least pull it back, because he was close to being out of regulation. But Troylus brushed the hair back into his eyes, covering them from the gazes of the people he was passing. All they would notice was him rudely ignoring their smiles and hellos. Nothing new there.

At least the years of being pissed off at everyone had paid off in that no one expected him to be happy and shiny.

He found himself in the terrarium, sitting on the edge of the orchard, running his fingers through the soil packed around the roots of all the trees. A butterfly flew past his face and landed on the knuckles of his hand, its wings folding and unfolding, revealing a different pattern with each movement.

"Troylus," Indigo, his sister, said, "what are you doing here?"

"Just, um," he sat up straighter and turned to look at the tree, so his eye wasn't in her direction, "needing a break from everything. Did you hear about the baby?"

"It's terrible." Indigo shook her head and leaned against her spade. "What happened to the womb?"

"What do you mean?" he asked.

"Something must have happened to it; otherwise the baby would have lived, right? You're friends with Zellendine. I thought you would know."

"Not," he faltered, unsure how to go about answering that. Yes, he should know. He should have asked when he spoke to her instead of worrying first about whatever was going on with his eye. "Not as far as I know. She's been busy looking into it. I'm sure she and Stephen will figure it out."

"I just hope they do it fast. Things like that shouldn't happen." Indigo straightened up and leaned toward him, her face coming alight and a smile spreading on her lips. "Something extraordinary happened here; do you want to see?"

"Sure," he said, standing and brushing off the seat of his jumpsuit.

Indigo lead the way into the trees, leaving him to climb the short wall he'd been sitting on and trot after her.

Around a bend, they came to a nest in the tree branches overhead. Indigo put her finger to her lips and stepped carefully onto a low stool to peer over the edge of the nest. She smiled and stepped back, waving him forward.

Troylus climbed onto the stool and looked into the little basket of sticks and fluff, two baby birds were in it, their mouths wide open and craning their little necks upward.

He stepped down, his own mouth hanging open like the birds.

Indigo waved him after her as she gave the nest some distance.

"When–" he started, but she put her hand on his arm and stared around the tree back toward the babies.

"Just watch," she said.

They stayed frozen, staring at the nest as a bird flew to it and dropped into it, feeding her babies from her own mouth.

"We knew they could, but the birds have never done this before. We always had to take the eggs, incubate them, and feed them before releasing them again. Now, they're doing it on their own." Indigo looked like she did when they were small and she won a game they were playing. He hadn't seen the light in his big sister's eyes so bright since.

"But, what does that mean? Why are they doing it now?" he asked, his voice low and his brow furrowed.

"I don't know. Maybe they can feel how close we are to being on a planet again."

They were still a long ways from being on their new home, and the life of a bird was too short for the babies in the nest to ever see it. But he hoped Indigo was right, that this was a sign that their arrival on the planet was going to work out.

7

ZELLENDINE

THE GATHERING ROOM WAS ONE OF THE MOST RAMSHACKLE spaces on the ship. Not a single surface was without a patch of some kind. Even the window had bracing criss-crossing over a piece struck by space debris some time in the last hundred years while she had been asleep.

It was a shame the window was a mess now; it was one of the largest, offering some of the best views on the ship. Zellendine watched as a solar flare from the distant sun tickled the edges of the scene outside, the window automatically filtering the light in a way that allowed her to see the variations of heat and intensity in the ray, transforming it from a shard of light too bright to look at directly, to a work of the brightest art.

The leadership team sat on the floor in a loose circle, it reminded her of the classrooms she had spent so much of her early childhood in. But this circle held an air of solemnity that her classroom never did.

For herself, Zellendine didn't know if she should sit among them or not. She remained by the wall, standing with her hands tucked behind her back and chewing on her bottom lip.

"We have some Chapters business to deal with before we get to the reports about yesterday," Alara, the head of communications, said, brushing aside her thick, grey dreadlocks.

She was the one Zellendine thought of as their leader, not the captain of the ship who just steered them to their destination around whatever space had to throw at them. Alara, with her ageless dark skin and long grey dreads was always the one to make the announcements to the ship during their shift. Her heavy, honeyed voice was calming, even now when it held the weight of the stars.

"I have been in contact with the other Chapter ships, until last shift when Chapter ship twenty-seven was about to land on their assigned planet. Their comms have gone silent," Alara said, to the general intake of breath of the listening crowd.

"Do any of the other ships know what happened? Did they land?" The captain asked.

Alara shook her head, dropping it so her dreads fell forward again.

"No, none of them have heard from them since their spindle left the ship. It was mostly a water covered planet, but from all accounts their terraforming started well. We just have no idea what caused us to lose contact."

The spindle was an interconnected section at the center of the wheel which separated into seven pieces for landing on their assigned planet. Occasionally, one of the sections of a spindle wouldn't make it, but an entire ship? Zellendine couldn't remember such a thing happening and shook herself to put away remembrance; it wasn't part of moving forward.

"Even worse, Chapter ship twelve has apparently crashed into a space object sometime in the last shift."

Shocked exclamations chorused throughout the room.

Zellendine's knees felt weak, like she was in the center of the ship where the gravity produced by the turning of the wheel shape was lessened.

Was this something that happened often and no one outside leadership knew? That couldn't be the case, her father would have said something.

"How do you know it was a crash? Maybe they lost comms too." One of the voices clamoring to be heard over the uproar managed to clearly get their point out.

"The crew successfully sent out a distress signal." The room fell silent as Alara spoke.

Zellendine leaned forward to hear her more clearly, holding her breath so she didn't miss anything.

"Chapter ship three got the signal and has been trying to make sense of all of it and let the rest of the fleet know. They report the message is damaged somehow. I don't know anything more."

"Are we still going to make our landing on schedule?" Zellendine's father asked.

"Yes, we aren't scrapping the mission. We still need to colonize this planet, and so far, the scans suggest minimal terraforming and no lifeforms that will be challenges to us. But it does mean that moving forward, we all need to be aware of the risks and take the necessary precautions. We need to have the time to make major repairs to the Wheel before we can attempt to make another trip anywhere near the length of the one we just took," Alara said, each person in the room nodded.

No one aboard the Wheel could miss the rickety hallways, or the mismatched patches. And the stains of thousands of years of human activity made the whole ship look dingy and muted. They needed more supplies to restock, and a ship rebuilt from proper parts, not rigged together out of whatever they could spare. There was even an old bunk frame that had been torn apart for a repair on one of the doors into engineering.

"Always move forward, sometimes means taking a minute to fix things so we don't stop moving at all," the lead of the starwalkers said to a small smattering of laughter.

Zellendine smiled too, any comic break from the heavy news, even at the expense of their ship, was welcome.

And the starwalker would know. His crew was kept busier than most just to keep the outer hull together and repair the times space decided to throw things at them, which was often.

"Now, I understand we have something of an emergency onboard this ship. Stephen? Can you enlighten us?" Alara said, turning to Zellendine's father.

"First, Zellendine was attending the birth yesterday and has been working with robotics on the womb, so I'll let her update everyone," her father said.

The room full of eyes turned toward her and a lump lodged in her throat.

"Okay," Zellendine said, taking a breath to control the sweat that was starting to collect in the small of her back.

"Come here, please. You don't need to stand by the door." Alara waved her over to the space next to her.

Zellendine made pushed off the wall and headed to Alara, picking her steps carefully as she navigated through the scattered people.

Once she took her place, and Alara and Stephen nodded in her direction, she told everyone what happened in the birthing room and the lack of answers they had been able to find to explain it.

"Stephen?" Alara asked, her face going from shock to confusion and back.

"I'm wondering if this has happened before," her father said.

People around her shifted in their places, some crossing their arms and grumbling under their breath things she couldn't make out.

Alara waved her hand, tamping down the reaction before it could get too large. "Why do you think you should look backward? We are always moving forward."

"I know, but if this happened before, any other shifts might not pass along the information during the transfer thinking it was a rare occurrence, a unique malfunction. In order to see if there is a pattern, and if that would give us an answer as to why this happened, I'll need to look back," Stephen explained.

Alara nodded her head and the faces of the people around her looked a degree less angry.

"Could you think of a way to find out if there is a pattern and not defy the mandate?" Alara asked.

Stephen hesitated, his jaw flexing and eyes on his lap.

Zellendine shifted in her place, some of the people who still wore their anger like a starwalking suit that covered them head to toe, were glancing at her.

"We could tell the next shift to watch for it happening and that they need to warn the next shift and so on," Stephen said.

His words were like a stun gun being shot into the hearts of the people in the room. All of them froze, some with their mouths hanging open.

The captain was the first to drop his head as he said, "People will panic."

"We need to put births on hold until we land, then," Alara said.

"Many partners have been waiting for their last shift, or the approach, so that they wouldn't have to abandon the surface for two years in order to have a child," Zellendine blurted out and felt her cheeks heat up in a blush as the room full of people laughed.

"Zellendine, when we land people will be able to have children the old-fashioned way," Stephen said.

"But what about the partners who don't have sperm or a womb?" she asked.

"Hmmm," Alara said, nodding her head. "You're right. We should let people know the risks and proceed as they choose."

The conversation moved on but Alara kept her eyes on Zellendine, her gaze appraising, and unnerving.

8

———

TROYLUS

Inside his suit in space, Troylus struggled with the last of the sealant he had to coax into the seam of the old patch of the terraforming office's window. A bubble of the stuff floated past his helmet, but the rest was doing as he wanted, working its way into the brittle crack of the old sealant.

He said a silent thanks to whoever the person was who came up with the formula for them to make the stuff on board the ship. The rest of the passengers may not have realized it, but all starwalkers knew that the ship would have fallen apart a long time ago without it.

Troylus ran his gloved hand over the place he had just worked on, pulling his fingers back when he was done to make sure nothing was on his glove. A job well done.

"All finished out here," he said into his mic. His earpiece crackled to life a second later.

"Come on in, then. Everyone else is already gone for the day," Rullon said from inside the office.

Of course, his dad stayed until Troylus was done; it was

what they did for each other. While the rest of the crew might kick off early, Troylus and Rullon usually didn't unless they both could. It was one of the only positive things about him getting the starwalking assignment, he got to work closely with his dad.

Troylus pushed off from the hull and let the turning of the ship bring the airlock back into view. He grabbed a handhold as it passed and pulled himself into the airlock. Pushing the button to reel in his tether, then the other button to close the door behind him and stepped into the interior chamber while the effect of the turning ship's false gravity pushed into his body, he closed his eyes for a moment. Troylus opened his eyes again and pulled the lever to close the second door between him and the vastness of space.

The vents into the small chamber hissed as they filled it with air and Troylus's heart finally slowed back to normal. No matter how many times he went out to do some repair or another, his heart rate reminded him that it was dangerous as fuck. It had only been two shifts since one of the other star-walkers had died.

Rullon always said how much he was going to miss it once they landed, but Troylus was thrilled at the prospect of never having to risk space again.

Just one more stasis.

The light over the inner door turned on and Troylus opened it, closing it again behind him before he took off his helmet and gloves, breathing deeply of the air inside. He supposed the faint smell of sweat when he was enclosed in his suit wasn't all bad, but it sure as hell wasn't great.

He took off the rest of his walking suit, hanging it in its place, and joined Rullon in the small office.

"Any flags?" he asked, as he always did, although they were so often surprised by the objects that collided with them, or the repairs that popped up, he wasn't sure why he checked anymore.

"Nope, nothing showing for the next few days, anyway." Rullon pushed his chair back from the holo and smiled at him.

"Get out of here, Troylus. Find something fun to do."

"What will you do?" he asked as Rullon passed him into the corridor.

"I'm going to get something to eat and go to bed early," he said over his shoulder with a half-hearted wave.

Rullon was more tired than usual, but Troylus wasn't sure why. He and his dad were close, but not close enough for him to pry.

The ship lurched and a grinding sound reverberated through every surface around him.

"What the hell was that?" he asked no one.

He checked the holo and didn't see any flags pop up to explain any external hits. The ship regularly lurched or made some strange noise that moved through everything no matter where it emanated from. It was almost always either a strike from space or something happening in the engine, but this one was worse than others he remembered.

Without anything else to entertain him, he decided to check up on engineering; it definitely wasn't a strike.

The smell of lubricant and hot metal wafted down the hall so Troylus smelled engineering long before he reached it.

From outside, he could see into the room full of a tangled maze of metal that spidered out into the walls to feed into the rest of the ship. In the center of the mass was the glowing core of the engine's power source. None of the engineers seemed even remotely concerned, they weren't running around. Two were even leaning up against a wall and smiling, one had her head thrown back in laughter.

Whatever had made the ship lurch must not have been that

big of a deal. Strange, because he would have sworn it was far more than the usual hiccup. Troylus decided to get something to eat and visit Briar asleep in his tank. He was obviously too messed up about his eye and Zellendine's dismissal if his perception was that far off.

9

ZELLENDINE

AFTER PLACING THE SMALL PACKAGE CONTAINING THE unfortunate baby in an ejection hatch, Zellendine closed the door. Her heart was in her throat and her eyes were threatening to betray her lack of professional distance to Stephen standing next to her. She pushed the button to send the child into the stars, gone forever from their ship.

Heedless of the breach in decorum, because her heart demanded it, she placed a hand on Anders and Yanna's shoulders where they stared out the small window, watching as their only child was sent into the arms of the universe.

"Why did this happen?" Yanna asked no one. She had been repeating the question all day.

"Yanna, please go rest," Anders said, trying to pull her away.

"If you need anything..." Stephen said, letting the rest of his sentence hang, before he tapped Zelledine on the elbow and made his way from the hallway.

A hallway wasn't the kind of place Zellendine would have designed for a final goodbye, but the builders of the Wheel either hadn't planned on death being something they would have to deal with, or it was part of only moving forward, there wasn't time enough to mourn in any other way but moving from one point to another. The intention of the builders wasn't something people asked about. It was too long ago.

No moving backward, only forward, Zellendine reminded herself. Besides, there was more than enough happening right now to focus on.

She had not had a chance to talk it through with Stephen and she wanted to understand, to know if there was something she missed. The vitals had looked good. She would have sworn everything would be okay.

"Stephen, do you think it's the process of getting samples?" Zellendine asked once they were a far enough distance that the couple in mourning wouldn't hear them.

"No. We've used samples gained from the same processes for many couples. This is something different. The child had no cellular reason for not surviving..." he trailed off.

"You said in the gathering that we should warn people, but what do we say? That we have a possibility of a fifty percent infant mortality rate?" she asked, her voice pitched low in case someone else was in earshot.

She stopped in her tracks, the implication of what she just asked running through her mind.

Her steps rang against the uneven and worn soft wood floor of the hallway as she ran to catch up to him.

"It's the only thing we can do, Zellendine. All we can hope is that people remain calm and think through any decisions," Her father's voice was solemn and bewildered, his eyebrows knit together, and his mouth pinched.

"And we've only had one birth this shift," Zellendine said. "Only one couple will be spending the next shift awake. If it continues once we're on the planet, that's..." There were no words Zellendine could think of that were strong enough for the tragedy of an ongoing rate of death that high.

"Before we say anything, I'm looking into these sudden problems. Don't worry, I'm sure we'll figure out why this is happening before the next shift," her father said, but his face hadn't changed, and Zellendine couldn't help thinking that he didn't believe it himself.

There was only a month left until the next shift, this was their last period awake before the final approach when the entire population of the Wheel would come out of cryogenic sleep, one hundred years away.

No one else would even think to look back to previous shifts like he had suggested. No one else would make the attempt to fix whatever problem killed this baby. It wasn't the way of the people of their ship. This was on her father. And it was on her to help him.

"At least this happened now, and not thousands of years ago when we started this journey." Zellendine realized after the words left her mouth that Stephen was too far ahead to hear her. She swallowed, hard, and reminded herself to stop thinking about the past.

Shifts lasted one year, every one hundred years, with just enough people awake to keep the ship going while the others remained in stasis. Zellendine couldn't imagine how any of the medics would have had enough time to even attempt to find a solution. She was almost done with her apprenticeship, and the amount of time it took to do anything medical was still something she was coming to grips with.

Zellendine knew her dad would put himself through hell to figure it out.

Walking along the hallway, she passed the spoke to the medical bay, where her father was headed. She continued on to one of the cryo bays, the one she visited most often.

Steps from the door, the whole ship rattled and lurched, she caught herself on the wall.

"Damn it," a voice from within the room said and muttered about engineering getting their shit together.

Zellendine knew that voice but couldn't imagine what it was doing in the cryo bay.

"Troylus," she said, her voice whipping into the room from the hall, "what the fuck? Are you trying to start a fight again? Here?"

In the middle of the grey room, Troylus rolled his eyes and leaned back from where he was bent over the lowest cryo tank in the stack of four in front of him.

"Fine," Troylus said. He stood and made his way to the opposite door before turning back and sneering at Zellendine. "But when Briar wakes up, no matter what you think is going to happen, he and I are going to talk and there will be changes coming, so hang on to your friendship while you can, Zellendine."

"Stop, Troylus," Zellendine yelled at her friend's back.

Troylus didn't turn around, but at least he stopped walking.

"This doesn't make sense." Zellendine softened her voice to the one she used on the small children she saw at the clinic. "Why are you so mad at me? It's like you came out of stasis already pissed off and I don't know what I did. We're supposed to be friends."

"Maybe when Briar wakes up, you'll understand," Troylus said over his shoulder, "but not if I tell him what you did first." He stormed out of the room and all Zellendine could do was watch him go and rage inside her mind.

Whatever was going on with Troylus, she would deal with it later. She couldn't handle the stress right after the scene in the hallway and the news she heard at the gathering.

Zellendine curled her hands into fists and stalked to the seat she considered hers, next to Briar's cryo tank.

She put her hand, still balled into a fist, on the glass over his chest.

"Hey, Briar," Zellendine said. "I know I'll see you in a couple days, but some weird stuff is going on and…"

And, what? Zellendine wasn't sure. Just that she always went to Briar with her troubles. Even when he wasn't awake.

When Briar's dads had another baby and spent an extra year awake to bond, putting them in the same shift as Zellendine and her parents, he had become an integral part of her life. When they were seventeen, three years ago, his dad's surprised everyone by having another baby and sending the entire family into the following shift.

Last shift, as a joke during the transfer, some of the people around their age started talking about who they would partner with. Briar said her, but she had laughed it off. Was that why Troylus was so mad at her? Did he think she was being cruel to his friend?

She wanted to partner with Briar, but she had made the decision a long time ago not to partner until they landed. Most of the people her age said the same during their ridiculous partner conversation. And based on the ages of the people having babies, she assumed it was true. Maybe other people were partnering, just not having children. It happened a lot, but social commitments weren't recorded, and people changed their partners as they needed.

But she didn't want to change partners either. She wanted Briar. For more than the short time they got during transfers.

"I miss you, Bri," she said, her hand open against the glass. "This is the last shift. Then we'll be landing."

She looked out toward the stars beyond the window, wondering exactly how many they had passed in the generation since they left their last colony planet. A planet Zellendine's parents left when they were young. She shook her head, reminding herself that none of that mattered. It was all in the past.

"What do you think this one will be like?" she asked of her silent, sleeping friend.

The favorite pastime of most people on board was to wonder about the new world they were headed to, how much terraforming they would need to perform, if there would be any animals that called it home.

"It would be nice if there's no terraforming. I know you might like it, but it would mean more waiting. I think we all need to get off this old clunker for a while."

TROYLUS

Troylus rubbed his fist over his face as he stormed away from the cryo bay. Damn it, why did she get to him so bad?

She didn't do anything, but he wanted his words to sting. To hurt. When she yelled at him, because she didn't know he visited Briar too and she clearly didn't like it, he had lashed out.

But what had he even said? It was some kind of threat and that didn't make any sense. He couldn't even remember his words, just the feeling of the blood pounding loud in his head.

Yes, he had every right to visit his friend too, but it wasn't her fault she didn't know he did it. He never told anyone and tried to keep it from her. Since their awkward foray last shift into partner plans, he didn't want to see that look pass across her face again. The one she wore when she looked at him like she pitied him. It seemed like every time he saw her lately, he was overcome with anger. It filled him. Even after walking so far from the cryo bay, his footfalls were still heavy and his fists still clenched.

Troylus leaned against the wall and stretched his fingers out, taking deep breaths. He couldn't keep doing this with her. He was going to have to apologize. Again. Damn it.

He hated apologizing. Not the act of humbling himself to admit he was wrong, that part was easy. Everyone was wrong sometimes. He hated apologizing because he wanted to be better, to not need to apologize. Especially when he wasn't apologizing for just not knowing something or making a basic mistake, but this was going to have to be admitting he acted like a dick. And he should have been better than that.

Cara and Tessa walked by with their baby in a wrap Tessa was wearing.

"Hi, Troylus, what are you up to?" Cara asked, stopping to talk to him while Tessa swayed and looked down at the baby shaped bundle on her front.

"Oh, just thinking. Is the baby sleeping?" he asked, smiling at them.

"No; do you want to see?" Tessa asked, leaning so he could peer into the wrap at the tiny face inside.

The baby blinked up at him with golden yellow eyes which were a striking color he had never seen before.

"Beautiful eyes," he said, glancing back at Tessa and Cara, neither of whom shared the trait, although the baby had the rich dark brown skin Cara did.

"Thank you," Cara beamed, and Tessa smiled.

"We thought," Tessa said, "well, the computer said the eye color would be brown like Cara's. I suppose yellow is on the spectrum of brown?"

They all smiled and marveled at the baby before he said goodbye and headed toward his living quarters, wondering how the DNA would say brown and have it manifest as actually golden yellow. He didn't know all the vagaries of DNA, just the basics like everyone else since he wasn't a medic, but it seemed odd.

Opening the door to his living quarters, he found Rullon's large bunk was shut tight. His dad really had gone to bed early. His own bunk was small, and he barely fit into it anymore, but his dad used to share a bunk with his mother, and he had earned the extra space.

Troylus grabbed a bite from the service, the hard, dry bar reminding him he needed to pick up fresh rations, and sat at their small table.

When his mother was alive, their tiny cabin was a place of warmth and positivity, but since the accident it felt frozen, stuck, waiting for her to walk through the door.

Another family used their same cabin when they were in stasis, but the place remained regulation, nothing marking it as the same space they occupied for every shift of their lives.

His sister's cabin, the one she moved to after she got her partner, had little touches she put up every shift and carefully packed away before she went back into the tanks. He looked around and wondered where Rullon had packed the items his mother always decorated and put away like his sister did. He hadn't thought about them in many shifts. Instead, he just followed his father's lead and kept moving forward like he was told.

Troylus drank some water and flopped into his small bunk, berating himself for allowing the asinine edict of the ship to let him push aside the memory of his mother.

Itching his eye, he realized his head was buzzing and his hands were shaking.

First, he had out of control anger whenever he looked at Zellendine, and now this. He shook out his hands and curled up on his side. It had to stop. He was going to have to see Stephen and get checked. Because something was wrong, and he hated feeling out of control of himself.

11

ZELLENDINE

"Turn your head for me, Troylus, and look at the letters on the wall," her dad said, shining a light into Troylus's now partially silver eye.

"What do you think it is, Stephen?" Troylus asked him, while Zellendine tried to busy herself with entering Troylus's vitals into the holochart because she didn't want to show her lack of distance in front of her dad.

Her dad knew her too well, he would see right through to her growing irritation with Troylus.

"Your sight isn't changing, and all your nerves, retina, and blood supply look fine," Stephen said, turning a dial on the light in his hand. "I don't think it's anything to worry about. If it remains like this, I think we'll just assume it's something harmless in your DNA."

"Harmless?" Troylus asked.

"As long as it's not taking your sight, yes." Stephen cocked his head at Troylus.

"Well, it's taking my eye *color*. That isn't nothing." Troylus's voice was like a glove snapping onto a hand, fast and sharp.

Zellendine swallowed. Troylus had been so volatile lately, and she didn't want this visit to the clinic to devolve into an argument.

"No, you're right," Stephen said, his voice like the one he used on Zellendine when she was young. "I'm sorry that's upsetting to you. Perhaps it will stop, and if it continues, I can do a DNA test. But, of course, I'll keep looking for an answer."

Troylus humphed and stared at Zellendine, like it was her fault her father didn't care about Troylus's stupid eyes changing color.

The silver was prettier than the green he had to start with anyway. It looked like a star was shining out of a quarter of one of his eyes. Zellendine had brown eyes and Briar had grey, but they didn't shine like the changed part of his.

"I'll look in your chart and in the literature for an explanation, okay?" her dad asked and Troylus nodded, stepping down from the exam table and making his way out of the room without so much as a goodbye.

"You need to talk to him," her dad said, walking out himself and leaving Zellendine to finish the notes in the chart.

Fine, she would talk to Troylus. But first, she had somewhere she needed to be.

She looked at the clock on the holo and typed faster. She wouldn't be late. Not today.

After she was done, she took off her gloves, washed her hands, and darted from the clinic, weaving her way around an engineer walking the hall.

"He won't be happy if you break an arm falling on the way," the engineer said to her back, laughing.

She laughed and waved behind herself at him as she picked up speed.

Making her way into the cryo bay she was aiming for, she took a relieved breath and leaned against the wall. The room was buzzing with the activity of the stasis team as they moved among the tanks doing their work.

Once they were done with their check, one of them waved her forward and she went to her seat next to Briar's tank.

Every single time he had woken up since he went to the following shift, she wassitting by his side, and every single time she had gone to sleep since the shift change, he was next to her.

The glass on his tank was already starting to lose its frosted look, growing more clear and allowing her to see all the details of his face instead of just the vague outline and the color of his skin and hair.

A few minutes later, a swooshing sound accompanied the opening of the tank, the top half sliding down over the bottom half and exposing him to the air for the first time in one hundred years.

Zellendine reached into the tank and took one of his hands in hers, brushing his hair off his forehead with the other hand. His skin was already warm again.

She waited while his breathing sped up and his eyelids started to move. Around her, the people waking up in the other tanks started the small movements that always preceded their full waking.

Briar's hand gripped hers and he tossed his head to the side, not yet quite conscious.

"Good morning, Bri," she said. "I missed you."

"Zelle," he muttered, his eyes still shut, but he stopped thrashing his head and calmed, his hand softening the grip on hers and his thumb brushing against her knuckle.

Stasis crew made their rounds, checking on the waking people and talking to each of them. One of the crew just stopped at the foot of Briar's tank and watched them for a minute, making notes in the holo he was holding. Letting hers be the voice to draw out her friend.

"How much did you miss me?" Briar asked, one side of his mouth quirking up.

Zellendine bit her bottom lip and tried to suppress a smile.

He opened one eye and grinned. "Are you going to show me?"

She felt her face heat with a blush and bit down harder on her lip.

"You've got to stop biting that lip and bring it over here," he said, his voice the exact same as it had been when he was teasing her before she went to sleep last shift.

For the first time in what seemed like a year, and was actually more than a centennial, regardless that the stasis crew were milling about, and the other members of Briar's shift were walking up all around them, including his family, she leaned into the tank and kissed him.

He sighed as she did and brought his other hand up to cup her cheek.

"I dreamed about you," he said as she pulled back to look at him.

"No, you didn't," she said, smiling and shaking her head at him. No one dreamed during stasis, they didn't have the brain activity for it. It wasn't actually like sleep, as much as they called it that.

"Yes, I did." Briar looked so serious, she almost believed him and asked about it, but he sat up and wrapped her in his arms, making her forget the question.

1 2

TROYLUS

His eye was worse. A lot worse.

Troylus rubbed at it with a knuckle and trudged down the corridor to the starwalker office.

Maybe he should have headed the other way to say hello to Briar and the others coming out of stasis, but he didn't want to be irrationally angry with Zellendine again and she would be there. He didn't know why one of the wombs malfunctioned and a baby died, why his eye was turning silver, or why he was fluctuating between rage at one of his friends and out of control panic at nothing, but he knew Zellendine would be sitting next to Briar and holding his hand as he woke up.

Sometimes he wished he had been the one to transfer shifts and then have friends to greet him when he woke up. All he got was the stasis crew doing their checks.

People passed him in the corridor, smiling and dipping their heads at him. He didn't respond. He usually didn't, but today everyone else was in high spirits, ready and eager to welcome the members of the next shift.

The starwalker office was over full, three of the others were jammed into the small space. Troylus furrowed his brow in confusion. Usually it was just his dad at the comms and maybe Maurice.

"What's going on?" he asked, poking his head into the room.

"Flags," Rullon said, not looking up from his holo.

"How many and what impact?" Troylus asked, the question routine, but the singular focus of the three people in the room wasn't. "And where's Parmita?"

"She's out there right now, finishing up a patch," Rullon said.

Maurice put his hand to his ear and the small input tucked into it.

"Parmita is headed to the airlock now," Maurice said and all of them relaxed.

Troylus didn't. None of them had answered the question.

"What impact are we expecting here?" he asked again, his hands gripping the edges of the doorway harder.

"It doesn't make sense." Rullon's voice was low and he still wasn't answering, but his muttering made the hairs on Troylus's arm stand on end anyway.

"Rullon?" he asked and heard the fear in his own voice.

"Troylus, we don't know how many or what trajectory and have no way to guess the impacts. I don't know how to answer you," Rullon said, turning to face his son.

"How do we not know how many?" Troylus squeezed himself into the room to look at the holos over the shoulder of the three people already staring at them.

Every now and then a flag came in too fast for them to see it coming and that was usually when the most damage was done, but to see the flag and not know anything about it... that didn't make any sense.

On the map of space directly around the wheel there was a wavering line in the path of the ship. It stretched from one side to the other and seemed to be changing and morphing with every beat of Troylus's heart.

"Call the captain," Troylus said, his voice hushed and shaking.

"Already did," Maurice said, shaking his head. "He says the anomaly goes too far in every direction; we have to go through it."

"Then call Alara. There's no way we can get through that. We have to change course, go back and find another way around the sun." Troylus couldn't believe they thought this wasn't going to be a complete disaster. Something that big, no matter how amorphous or how stationary, could destroy the ship. Even with the starwalkers from the next shift, if the ship was too damaged, they wouldn't have enough people to make the repairs. Whole sections of the ship could be forced to shut down and regular maintenance wouldn't get done shutting down even more sections.

"She is trying to work out a plan using all the astros and all their maps, but it looks like this damn thing goes all the way across this system," Rullon said.

Troylus made a thump sound as he dropped back to lean against the wall, afraid his legs wouldn't hold him up on their own.

All the way across the system. There was no way to get away from this thing without turning around and they were so close to their destination. The planet, their long awaited home, was just on the other side of that... thing.

Parmita ducked her head into the room and wiped a loose hair out of her eyes.

"I don't know why the map says that's there; I'm telling you, there's nothing," she said, shaking her head.

"Nothing?" Troylus asked and waved a vague hand at the holos.

"Nothing is reflecting the light of the sun at all and we're so close to the sun we would see that, right?" Parmita asked, leaning against the door jam.

Troylus was jostled away from the wall by the ship lurching and a grinding noise. Everyone else seemed not to even flinch.

"Did..." he started and stood up straight before finishing, looking around at his crew members, "did you all feel that?"

"Feel what?" Rullon asked and Parmita raised her eyebrow at Troylus, one corner of her mouth quirking up.

"Are you sick?" she asked.

"No, I..." He looked at all of them, each wearing the same questioning expression as his dad. Except Parmita, who looked like she was gloating. "Never mind." He slumped back against the wall.

"Well," Rullon said, turning back to the holos, "if we're going to head through this thing, we need to get some eyes out there and prep for damage."

13

ZELLENDINE

A STASIS CREW MEMBER RAN PAST, FOLLOWED BY ANOTHER, sprinting and shaking their holo.

"What's going on?" Zellendine asked and Briar looked around, rubbing his eyes, while some of the other members of his shift sat up in their tanks.

"They're all down at the last stack." Briar grabbed for the edge of the tank, pulling up his knees to climb out.

"No," Zellendine said, putting her hands on his shoulders. "You shouldn't try and walk just yet. You'll fall and hurt yourself. I'll check it out."

He kissed her and relaxed his legs back onto the soft cushion inside his cryo chamber.

She made her way to the last stack of tanks and the stasis crew was frantically running scans of the people still in the open tubes, with their eyes closed, and no signs they were waking.

"What's wrong?" she asked, her voice hushed and her hands starting to shake.

Briar's little brother was in the bottom tank, not moving.

"Oh, Zellendine, maybe you can help," one of the crew said, visibly relaxing. "All of their vitals are fine and say they should be waking up, but they're not."

He handed her the holo and she scanned the information that confirmed what he said, except…

"They're asleep," she said.

"Yes, that's what I said."

"No, I mean, they're in REM sleep. Real sleep." She looked up at him, his eyes had gone wide and his mouth hung open.

"But that…" he said, trailing off.

"Doesn't happen," she said, crowding into the narrow space between the tanks he was already taking up most of.

Crouching down to Briar's little brother, Upton, she placed her hand on his small chest.

His skin was warm through his shirt, his face peaceful with the flush of youth painting his cheeks in health. Outwardly, there was nothing wrong with him, so why was he asleep?

"Upton, buddy?" Zellendine said, jostling him a tiny bit. "Can you wake up for me? Briar is waiting for you. Daddy and Poppa are waiting for you. Rhea is waiting for you."

She ran through the names of his family, trying to get any response, even a groan. She had seen the little boy wake up from a regular nap before. It usually involved rolling away from the person trying to get him up, whining, and then exploding with energy and ready to go.

But Upton didn't do any of those things. He remained fast asleep, with no sign he would break out of it.

Zellendine checked the holo; he was still in REM. There wasn't even a blip while she spoke or shook him.

"I think we need to get his dads," she said, standing and handing the holo back. "And I'll get Stephen to come and check on all of them."

She went to Briar in his tank. He was twirling his feet around in circles and stretching out his arms.

Her heart was in her throat as she sat in the chair by his side.

"Let me help you get out of the tank," she said.

"But I should…" His voice trailed off as he looked at her, and he swung his legs over the edge.

"It's going to be fine, but we need to get your dads and your sister, and then I need to get my dad." She took his hand and helped him to his feet.

When someone woke up from stasis, it took time for their muscles to remember they were strong and for their joints to remember they could bend, so their walk to the end stack of tanks was slow.

"Upton is asleep, in deep REM, and he isn't waking up. The whole stack isn't. And we don't know why," she said, and felt the shiver move through his body as the color drained from his face.

For thousands of years, entering in and out of stasis was predictable; this was strange. This was wrong. She didn't have to drive it home. Briar knew.

He picked up his pace, and she kept her feet moving, letting him lean more on her so they could go faster safely.

"Please get my family," he said as he sat on the edge of his little brother's tank.

Zellendine nodded to the stasis crew member who went off to get them, while she went in the other direction to get her dad.

He would know what to do. He had to. Because no one else did.

1 4

—————————

TROYLUS

"I'll do it," Troylus said, standing away from the wall and taking a step before Rullon grabbed him by the arm.

"No, Troylus, let me," Rullon said, standing with his jaw set.

But the hand on his elbow shook, ever so slightly, and Troylus put his palm over his dad's.

"Rullon," Troylus started, and had to swallow back the urge to refer to him as Dad. "It won't take long. I'll be fine. And I want you here on the comms for me."

Troylus felt the eyes of the other starwalkers on them. It was a weight, like returning to the gravity of the ship after being in space. Their gazes pushed down on his spine, strengthening his need to get this done. After what happened to his mom, there was no way he would stand in this office and listen while something happened to his dad.

He let go of Rullon and stalked out to put on his suit.

Parmita followed and in silence helped him don his gear. She had a face that fluctuated between amusement and sardonic appraisal, but her face didn't look like that as she helped him.

53

She looked concerned and determined. Or maybe he was projecting his own thoughts onto her.

"Make it quick, Dumbass," she said, smiling, after he had his helmet on and she did the check of his suit, looking closely for any places it might leak.

"Oh, please. I'll be fine. You can't get rid of me that easy, Princess," he said, using the old nickname he had given her when he was new to the crew and she complained about getting her hair caught in her helmet. But his voice quavered, and he turned away before he had to speak to her again.

He pushed the button on the side of his helmet, it beeped back at him and he knew Rullon heard an answering beep in his ear piece in the office. Their comms were connected, but Troylus had zero intention of keeping them connected if, well, he wasn't going to think about the if.

The airlock took time to cycle through each door, until Troylus was floating into space, tethered to the ship by a thin line he clipped on his side. He controlled his trajectory by snagging one of the regularly placed handles on the outer hull of the ship. Some of the other starwalkers used the small bursts of air projected from their boots to do most of their walking, but he only used them when absolutely needed. It was a drain on the suit's air supply and his habit of ragged breathing while out there never sat right in his mind combined with using the bursts. All he had to do was touch a button on his arm to activate them, but instead, he hauled himself along the spinning side of the ship, hand over hand.

"Alright," Rullon said into the comm link. "Make this quick, okay?"

"Yep," Troylus answered, pulling himself from one hold to another along the hull, against the rotation, toward the front of the ship, his tether rolling out behind him.

Once he got into position, he let go of the hull and stayed as the ship moved past him. He turned around to see what the flag was picking up.

Nothing. He saw nothing to make sense of the readings on the map.

Whatever the anomaly was, it supposedly spanned the system. He turned, looking further into the dark of space, away from the bright light of the sun.

Parmita was right, there was nothing reflecting the light out there. Whatever was being picked up on their map, it blended into the dark. On the comm, Rullon was speaking to the others in the office, not bothering to sever the connection so Troylus heard them discussing how much time they had until the outer bands of the shifting anomaly found the ship.

He twisted to look the other way, from the dark of space toward the sun and… There. What was that?

15

ZELLENDINE

HER DAD WAS IN THE CLINIC, WRAPPING UP THE FOLLOW UP CHECK on the surviving baby. Stephen gave Cara and Tessa their instructions as he went over the place they could find answers to most of their questions in their holos.

She loitered in the doorway, shifting from foot to foot, until he caught her eye.

They said goodbye and nodded to her on the way out, her father waited for the door to close behind them before he stood and said, "What's going on?"

"Stasis problem," she said, filling him in on the details. He grabbed a bag and tucked his holo under his arm, running out the door with her and back to the cryo bay.

Every member of Troylus's family, and the families of the three other people still asleep, were crowded around the last stack of tanks, leaning against each other, the walls, and the tanks around them while their bodies gained strength.

They made room for her and her dad, who went to work checking each person, their tank, and running all the tests they could.

Zellendine squeezed Briar's hand every time she passed him while she worked, hoping she would be able to fix this. To save his brother from whatever this was.

Eventually the families were convinced to go to their living quarters, to eat and sleep, and hope that in the morning things would be back to normal.

"I'm staying," Briar said. Standing tall, his muscles and his will long since waking up all the way.

"You can't; your body needs food and sleep, and Upton is in good hands," his dad, Journo said, looking to Zellendine and her dad, rubbing a hand over his face.

None of them wanted to leave the cryo bay, Zellendine was sure about that, but Journo was right. After waking from cryo, they couldn't push themselves too hard, and there were basic human needs that had to be tended to.

"Dad," Briar said, "I'm in good hands too. I'm staying." He hugged both his dads and his little sister before turning back to Zellendine and her father and taking his place in the chair they had moved into place next to Upton.

"Journo, don't worry," Zellendine said. "I'll make sure he does what he needs to. Let me talk to him."

He gave her a wan smile and left with Rhea and his partner. She took a deep breath before turning back to Briar. He made a sad sentinel watching over the eerie silence of the four people stuck in their dreams.

Briar needed a break, and more than that, he did need to eat something. She snagged on her dad's sleeve as he walked by and gestured to her friend. Stephen took him in and sighed.

"Okay," her dad said before he handed her his holo. "I'll go get us something to eat, but take care of him." Stephen shook his head and left the cryo bay.

"Hey," Zellendine said, crouching in front of the chair. "Bri, I will figure this out."

Briar looked up at her, his eyes scanning her face and said, "I know you want to, Zelle. But this doesn't happen. How do you even know where to look?"

She didn't have a good answer for him, they didn't really know where to look, so they were left looking at everything which almost amounted to looking at nothing.

"Come on," she said, standing and holding out a hand to him.

"Zelle, I mean it. I'm staying here."

"I'm not trying to take you away, I just want to show you something." He allowed her to grab his hand and pull him to his feet. His arms wrapped around her and she hugged him back before taking his hand again and tugging him to the window.

"Space?" Briar asked, half his mouth quirking up at her. "I've kind of seen this before."

"Very funny," Zellendine said, bumping him with her shoulder. "No, look."

Tendrils of solar flares were licking at the edge of the view out of the wall filled with window.

"What is that? Are we passing a nebula?"

"I forgot for a minute that you just woke up," she said, shaking her head that with everything going on he had forgotten how close they were to their new home, and she had forgotten to remind him.

"Oh, yeah," he said, wrapping his arm around her shoulders and smiling. "I can tell you really missed me."

She smiled and kissed him, showing him exactly how much she had missed him. The kiss was tender and his hands on her back felt weighted by sadness.

"That's our new star. The sun for our soon to be sky," she said, pulling back and looking out at the flares again.

He leaned toward the window, his eyes far away as he took in the beams of light that were their first encounters with the home they had been heading toward their entire lives.

"Make a wish," Zellendine said, her voice low and reverent.

Briar whipped his head toward her. They used to wish on the first star they saw when they woke up from their stasis together. They made a deal when his family changed shifts that they wouldn't wish on another until they could do so on the star they could call their own, and until they could do it together.

He smiled and squeezed her hand before they both turned and closed their eyes to make their wish.

She wished for the ability to figure out what had happened to cause the waking to go wrong, so she would be able to not just reverse the issue to save these people, but so that it would be prevented from happening again. She assumed he wished for the same.

The door opened to her father carrying a stack of food bins. She and Briar each took one from him and they sat on the floor by Upton's tank, eating a silent meal.

With each bite Briar's eyes grew heavier, his blinks longer and his hand bringing his food to his mouth took longer to do it.

After most of the food was gone, Briar's eyes closed, and his body started to slump. Zellendine caught him before he could fall, and Stephen helped her get him to his feet.

Briar slowly opened his eyes and focused on Zellendine's face.

"Please look after him," he said, before closing his eyes again.

"I'll take him to his quarters," Stephen said, taking the weight of Briar's leaning form on himself and turning away from her toward the door of the cryo bay.

16

TROYLUS

His heartbeat, always faster when he was outside the ship, picked up its pace. A lifetime in space had taught him well. If it was weird, be worried.

"Troylus?" Rullon's voice broke through and made his heart skip a beat.

"Yeah," he said. "I'm here, looking at it."

"Wait, you can see it?" His dad's voice was excited.

But Troylus didn't know how to explain what he was seeing. It wasn't like any other flag he'd ever witnessed. This wasn't a comet, an asteroid, a nebula, and it wasn't an ice ring or the ring of moons they'd had to detour around one time. This wasn't even visible. Not really.

"It isn't like anything we've seen before."

Rullon's hissing inhale sounded through the comm and in the background Troylus heard the mumbling of the rest of the crew.

"Tell me."

"I can only see it by the sun, because the light is wrong where it meets the Grimm Star. I don't know what this thing is."

The anomaly in front of him wavered where it met the light, the entire side of the sun was fuzzier, less distinct in his visor. With the filters in his helmet, he should have been able to see some of the individual solar flares coming off the sun, but it was all a blurry, undulating haze, somehow brighter than the heart of the star.

He described what he was seeing to Rullon who repeated every word to the rest of the team.

"You should put up as many shields as you can before we hit it and get back to the airlock," Rullon said, his voice hard.

"Okay," Troylus answered, turning back to the ship and pulling closed a shield over a window to a cryo bay. He worked furiously, sweat dripping down his back even though his suit stayed at a constant, cool temperature.

He had to protect the ship. In his head he repeated it. He had to protect the ship. Over and over again. As he slammed home shield after shield.

"Troylus," Rullon said. "Come on in now. We're getting close to the outer bands of this thing."

"I'm not done," Troylus said as he slammed home another shield.

"You're out of time." Rullon's voice was heavy with warning, and far too loud in the confines of Troylus's helmet.

The next window came into view, and through it he could see another cryo bay. And at the end of the stacks was Zellendine while Briar walked out the door with Stephen.

She turned toward the window and jumped when she spotted him on the other side, before she smiled and waved.

He raised a hand back to her and started to smile, but his comm blared to life, Rullon's voice reverberating through his helmet.

"Troylus, get out of there, now," Rullon yelled.

"What? Why?" Troylus asked, his waving hand grasping onto

the handle in front of him and Zellendine's face falling, her eyes squinting, and her head tilting to the side. She wasn't looking at him anymore, she was looking past him.

"The anomaly just spit something out. It's headed right for you," Rullon yelled.

"I have to shut this shield," Troylus said, making a grab for the large, ungainly piece of metal.

"No. Get in here. Now." Rullon's voice was hard and it made his heartbeat pound louder inside his head.

"But - " Troylus started, only for Rullon to yell into the comm so Troylus flinched and lost his grip on the shield again.

"Troylus, now."

Zellendine on the other side of the window widened her eyes and stepped back, grabbing onto the stack of tanks behind her, while her mouth dropped open and her other hand clenched around the front of her jumpsuit.

What the hell was she doing in there? Beyond her, Troylus spotted bodies still in their tanks, their eyes closed. On the bottom of the stack lay the small shape of Upton.

His stomach dropped into his feet and he made another grab for the handle of the shield.

"Troylus!" Rullon's scream echoed in his head as he turned to look back toward the anomaly.

In seconds, before his eyes, a plume of purple appeared out of the dark and took on shape. It formed into a hard, grey mass. Headed right at him.

17

ZELLENDINE

ZELLENDINE WATCHED IN HORROR AS A THING FORMED IN SPACE, over Troylus's shoulder.

She made eye contact with Troylus in his helmet. His eyes widened and his jaw clenched, his hand making wild grabs for something just out of sight.

"Get back," she yelled, waving her hand.

But he didn't retreat, he looked over his shoulder and doubled his efforts. His face took on a frantic determination and Zellendine pulled the tank's lid back over Upton, closing him in but not sending him back into stasis.

She climbed the stack of tanks, making her own panicked grabs and heaving the lids into place.

On the top of the stack her foot slipped, sending her piling up on the floor without closing the last lid.

Troylus looked over his shoulder and flinched back from the window as the object slammed into it.

Noise filled her head and Zellendine realized she was screaming.

But the window held, no matter how loud the impact was. It

held, but it was cracked. A large spot of white, shattered, yet intact glass in the middle of the window started to grow legs, the lines of them snaking out from the center in crazed and jagged patterns.

Zellendine crouched on the floor, her hands scrambling to pull herself up.

She climbed the stack of tanks again.

If she could just get the damn tank to close, all the people in the stack would have a chance to survive the window caving in. If she could do it fast enough, maybe she could get out before the window gave.

Troylus was waving his arms and gesturing wildly for her to leave.

But she had to help these people. They couldn't help themselves. They had no choice. They were stuck here.

Topping the stack, she heaved on the lid, harder than she needed to, it slammed closed while a high pitched whining sound emanated from the window.

She jumped to the floor just as the window gave, the first piece of glass separating from the rest. The sounds around her became loud and silent at the same time, like there was so much sound her mind stop processing it. She felt the air being sucked from her lungs and even though she couldn't hear it, she was vaguely aware she was trying to scream while everything happened in slowed down versions of seconds.

There wasn't time to get out. Zellendine fell to the floor and stared at Troylus. His face looked like he was screaming too. A blue light spilled out from him. And the window... fitted itself back together, the glass fusing itself back in place.

Zellendine's hands, gripped around the edge of one of the tanks, lost their ability to hold on, dropping to the floor in front of her as her mouth dropped open and her mind left her unable to make sense out of what she saw.

After the window was whole and perfect again, Troylus sagged against it, his face slack and his shoulders heaving. The void and totality of sound was gone. The air moved in and out of her lungs with little effort, although she was breathing in big gulping breaths.

He looked in on her and she stood up, drawn to stand before him.

Troylus was still breathing in heavy, body shaking breaths, but he put his hand on the window and smiled at her.

She smiled back, her mind screaming that she should be dead, that Troylus had saved her life. Through some kind of wish made reality, he had shown with light and fixed the window.

Behind her, footsteps pounded into the room; her dad was saying something, asking questions about her welfare and the closed tanks, but she couldn't really hear him. All she could hear was the blood still flowing through her and the question, how?

18

TROYLUS

HE COULDN'T CATCH HIS BREATH, BUT HE SQUEAKED OUT, "ALL clear," to Rullon on his comm and shut the shield on the cryo bay window although Zellendine was still looking at him.

Stephen stood behind her, his face puzzled as he talked. Troylus thought Stephen must have heard the impact.

But he couldn't think about the impact, he couldn't think much at all beyond wondering what just happened.

Troylus closed the last few shields and let himself float back to the airlock, his mind going back to the rage and fear he felt pouring from him in blue light that healed a broken window. The object, whatever it was, had disappeared as it had manifested, into purple and then nothing.

Looking at where the anomaly had shown itself, by the edge of the sun, Troylus now saw only the regular solar flares and moving of the star.

His comm was silent; Rullon must have turned it off, so Troylus pushed the button while the ship passed by him, its movement bringing the airlock closer to him.

"Rullon, what's the flag status?" he asked, snagging a hand

hold as it passed and pulling himself along toward his return to the safety of the interior of the ship.

"It's…" Rullon's voice trailed off before starting again, more sure and controlled. "We can't see it anymore."

Troylus stopped, hanging on the side of the turning ship as he looked at the place he had been able to make out the anomaly, the only place he could see it outside the map. Maybe Rullon was surprised it was gone, or he thought it was hiding, but Troylus wasn't and didn't.

Whatever it was, it seemed to come, do what it intended, and leave once he had done what he needed to. To protect the ship.

His heart wasn't pounding, it was more calm than it had ever been while starwalking, and he had just performed an act he didn't have a name for, but his mind was filled with the look on Zellendine's face as she stared through the window at him while it shattered between them. He couldn't hear her, but he was sure she was screaming.

Soundless through his helmet, her face, contorted in fear, nevertheless managed to make his whole body feel her screams.

The first airlock door shut behind him and he took his steps through the process while the gravity of the ship reclaimed his body. For the first time, the weight of his own body returning wasn't as welcome. For the first time, he wanted to be back out in space.

All the starwalker crew members were waiting for him as he walked through the last of the airlock doors and took off his helmet.

Parmita gasped and brought her hand to her mouth. Rullon squeezed his eyes shut and wrung his hands together before he grabbed Troylus in a hug, his body shaking.

Troylus hugged his dad back, but over Rullon's shoulder the rest of the crew were fidgeting and staring.

"What?" Troylus asked.

Did they get a sensor spike when the window was struck? Did they get another when it shattered? He thought they must have, but their reactions didn't make sense to him.

"Your…" Parmita started, but she didn't finish. Her incomplete statement hung in the air and Troylus wished he could read it out of the tension.

"Good job, Troylus." Rullon let him go and smiled, turning back to the crew with his hand resting on his son's shoulder.

Troylus read his father's unsaid words fine; he was daring them to have any other reaction than one of congratulations.

"I've never seen anything like that anomaly," Maurice said, a tremulous smile playing on his face. "Whatever it spat at you played havoc with our sensors, but you did well."

"Next - " Parmita stopped, licked her lips and put her face back into some semblance of her usual wry, teasing expression. "Next time, though, come in when you're told. We thought it was going to take you out."

He dropped his eyes and smiled, undoing his suit.

"We're almost home. I'll be happy if we never have another flag," he said, while Rullon helped him out of his gear.

"I closed all the shields and I think they should stay that way for a while until we know the anomaly isn't coming back." His words were met with solemn nods and he couldn't shake the feeling that these people, his crew, thought of him differently. But he was sure they didn't know what he had done out there. Hell, he didn't even know what he had done. Or what it meant.

19

ZELLENDINE

"Are you sure you're okay?" her dad asked after Troylus had shut the shield, his words finally breaking into her mind.

"Yeah," she said, turning back to look at her dad as she tugged her jumpsuit, straightening out whatever disheveled state it might have been in after her fall from the top tank. "Troylus was shutting shields and he scared me. He waved for me to get out of the room and I closed the tanks and fell from the top of the stack. It's nothing."

She stopped talking and bit her lip, aware she was rambling and trying to control her stammering. She didn't want to tell her father about what had just happened with Troylus. Not that she knew why, but even the thought of talking about the incident made her heart beat erratic and the hairs on her arms stand on end.

He looked at her with his eyes narrowed and his mouth pursed. She had to distract him.

"Now that the shield is closed, let's open the tanks back up and get to work."

His face cleared and he turned back to the stack and what they were in the cryo bay for.

"First, let's check their vitals while their tanks are shut. Maybe it will have some effect." Stephen attached his holo to one of the tanks and began to look through the information he received.

Zellendine did the same, forcing her hands to remain steady and her heartbeat to even out. It took her three times to register the information in front of her. Then she checked it again because it made no sense. The sleepers were all well according to the scans, their vitals were all steady and healthy, but they remained in deep REM.

"This is weird," Zellendine said, turning her holo so her dad could see it. "REM is inconsistent, they should be cycling through it, but they're just stuck in deep sleep with no change at all."

"Hmmm," Stephen said, his deep thinking noise that irritated Zellendine because it was almost always reserved for moments she would give anything for some damn words.

"Dad," she said, rubbing her hands over her face.

"Well, you're right. I don't know what this means, but we should do a check on the tanks themselves, I think. Make sure all their readings are calibrated." He climbed up to the top tank and began a scan.

She should have done the scan on Upton at the bottom, the little boy's chest rose and fell in regular, unending breaths but all she could think about was what she had just witnessed. All she could think about was Troylus. His face, the terror, pain, and rage that flashed across it before he put the world back together, and in the process, changed it completely.

Her mind wasn't equipped to deal with all the unanswered questions, she wasn't prepared to puzzle out why a baby died, why these people weren't coming out of stasis the way they always did, let alone what in the hell had happened with Troylus.

Zellendine had an errant thought pass through her mind and she stared at the empty tanks in the room. What if it had happened before, like her dad had suggested with the baby's death? What if the tank malfunction wasn't a one time occurrence? What if the window remaking itself wasn't the strange and unique moment she thought?

But, she couldn't say anything about it. Just thinking of the feat Troylus accomplished made her nauseous, so she swallowed that part down, but stepped to scan Upton in his tank while she tried to gain the courage to ask her father to break the law.

"Zellendine, I want to ask you something," her dad said, climbing down after scanning the occupants of the top two tanks while she was scanning the one above Upton.

"Yeah?" she said, her heart picking up its pace inside her chest. Please don't make me lie to you again, she begged him in her mind.

"What is going on with you and Troylus?" he asked.

Of all the things she thought he would say, that wasn't one of them.

"Nothing." Her voice tripped on the word as she continued to check the patient.

"Hmmm," he said.

She bit her lip and started to check the tanks themselves, to compare their data to the information her holo was picking up from the sleepers. Her fingers were less sure as she tapped out instructions, in her mind she screamed at her hands, forcing them to keep their shaking to a minimum.

"It seems like you two are having difficulty with your friendship this shift." Her dad was staring at the tanks and doing his own scans, but she didn't dare move her head to look at him, just peeked at him out of the corner of her eye. He was far too casual.

"Not really," she said, trying to match his casual tone.

"Are you sure there isn't something going on? Because after all the tension, now you're screaming when he's on the other side of the window and it's concerning."

Stephen wasn't going to let this go and she had no idea how to explain the screaming so he would accept her excuse and she wouldn't have to tell him she saw the impossible happen, or how to explain the rift that had kept her and Troylus apart all shift when they were supposed to be friends and she didn't understand it herself.

"We've just been busy with other things," she said, but her dad turned toward her, frowning.

"Maybe we need to check through the holos for any mention of problems that have happened before," she blurted, her voice was low, and it cracked on the word before. Her knees were weak, and she held her holo against her chest so he couldn't see it shake in her hands. She had just broken the law. Out loud.

2 0

———

TROYLUS

RULLON LED THE WAY TO THEIR QUARTERS IN SILENCE. IT GAVE Troylus time to stare at his hands and wonder if they were still alright, if they were changed somehow by what he had done.

They looked the same. They felt the same. All of him seemed whole and functioned the same as it always had, but what he did... he didn't have the words for it. And that scared the shit out of him.

Once they were inside their quarters, after the door slid shut, Rullon rounded on him. Troylus stepped back, his shoulders hitting the door.

"You need to look in the mirror," Rullon said, his face blank.

Troylus stepped to the small mirror in the wet room and choked on his own breath. Both of his eyes were completely silver.

He coughed and bent over the sink, bracing himself on the sides of it with his hands while his legs shook beneath him.

It took him minutes that felt like an age to control himself, he couldn't lose it in front of his dad. He didn't know what to say, and Rullon didn't need to be burdened with the same doubt and worry floating through Troylus.

"What happened out there?" Rullon asked from his bed, staring at the ceiling, when Troylus entered.

"I…" Troylus failed to think of anything to say, any possible way to assuage some of the concern he knew his dad felt.

"Did you eat? I'm hungry," Troylus said instead of offering a half assed explanation that he thought would just make Rullon worry more.

Rullon gave a heavy sigh and climbed from his bed, moving to the service machine in the corner.

"What do you want to eat?" Rullon asked over his shoulder, opening the door to stare at the food they had.

"The real question is, what is there?" Troylus slumped into a chair and put his head in his hands, rubbing his forehead.

"How about some noodles?" he asked, but didn't wait for an answer before he grabbed a container from the service and put it in the cooker.

"Perfect." Troylus lifted his head to find Rullon staring at him.

"You can tell me, Troylus. Anything," Rullon said.

"I know, Dad." And he thought he did. He thought Rullon meant what he said, but… "I just don't know what to say."

There, he said it, as much as he was comfortable with. Troylus made eye contact with Rullon and saw a small, concerned smile form on his dad's face.

"Okay." Rullon said, taking the noodles out of the cooker and grabbing utensils for each of them before bringing them to the table.

Rullon sat across from Troylus and handed him a utensil before scooping up some noodles with his own.

"That's it? Just, okay?" Troylus asked, his utensil waiting in his hand for him to remember it was there and he was supposed to be eating.

"Yeah," Rullon said around a bite. "As long as you know you can talk to me about it anytime, all I can do is wait until you do know what to say." He smiled and grabbed another bite.

Troylus grabbed a couple bites of his own, the tremor in his leg beneath the table lessening as he ate.

"Can you tell me one thing though?" Rullon asked.

"Uh," Troylus said, chewing his food and swallowing before answering, buying time. "I'll try." He couldn't promise anything more than that and Rullon nodded.

"Okay, why were you yelling Zellendine's name?" Rullon asked, setting down his utensil to make eye contact with Troylus.

"I… She…" Had he yelled her name? Troylus didn't remember, but he had to admit that it was likely he had screamed her name even though she couldn't hear him.

Troylus took a bite and stared down at the utensil in his hand, trying to think back to all that he could have said during the impact. His dad wasn't acting like he had any real idea beyond knowing something strange happened out there, but Troylus couldn't be sure.

"She was in the cryo bay with some people still in tanks and she was startled by seeing me." The lie tasted bad in his mouth, like when he desperately needed to wash his mouth after he woke up in the morning.

"Well," Rullon said taking his utensil to the deposit wash and dropping it in, "like I said, whenever you have the words and know what to say, let me know. I'll be here."

Troylus finished eating while Rullon got into his bed. As Troylus cleaned up after himself, all he could think about was the look on Zellendine's face after he fused the window back together. She looked awed, but he had saved her life, so that made some sense.

He wasn't sure what Rullon's face would look like if he ever managed to explain. And more than that, he wasn't sure he wanted to find out. He didn't want his dad to look at him differently.

21

ZELLENDINE

"Zellendine." Stephen's voice was low and weighted with warning. He went to the doors of the cryo bay, ducking his head out of each like he was scanning the halls, before he made his way back to her side.

"Do you think it's necessary?" he asked, his voice barely perceptible and his mouth moving in tiny fractions like he was afraid the walls could see him speak the crime. The people still sleeping in their tanks didn't hear him, so she wasn't sure what the point of the added layer of subterfuge was, although it did make her hands shake less.

"I'm starting to," she said, using his same tactics to speak. She was surprised to discover she wasn't lying. She did think going back and looking at previous shift's scans and logs would be helpful.

"Alara didn't approve my request to look back at any trouble with the wombs," Stephen said, his face screwed up as he stared into the middle distance at nothing.

"She's brilliant…" Zellendine started but had to bite her lip before continuing, her thought not charitable nor something she would have ever believed she would say, but a lot of what was unbelievable was happening. "But I think she's wrong." She said it nicer out loud than it was in her head.

Her father looked at her, his eyes examining her in much the same way Alara had in the meeting room. It made her itch with the need to squirm under his inspection. She had no idea what he was looking for.

"Okay," he said, his voice breaking the silence made her jump. "Let's check for previous tank malfunctions."

Zellendine breathed out a heavy sigh and slumped, her hands finally still.

"I'll do it," she said. "Keep looking through what data we have from these tanks right now."

She sat in the little chair and started scanning through the holo, unsure where to even look for what she wanted to find. The act of looking back wasn't something she did. No one did. Even in the clinic she had a file for each person they kept updated on current issues that held any information they needed about things that could possibly cause a problem for someone in the future. It even held stuff on childhood injuries because of the inflammation they could cause when someone was older. No file from the past had ever been needed. She didn't know where they were kept.

The holo in her hand was connected to all the files of all the crews on the ship, she started by getting into the stasis crew files and the medic crew files, trying to access the things those crews didn't bother to put into the current files.

It had to be somewhere, the information didn't just disappear, and she knew from her work in the clinic that not everything got into the current files. The stasis crew's files weren't what was most familiar to her though. They netted her nothing.

Next, she tried the medic files, the ones she knew better than anything else from her daily work. Scanning through files, trying to take her time so she could remember how she got into things and how to get back out again, she tapped away at her holo.

Hours passed with nothing to show for her efforts, but she was running out of options, so she felt energized by the hunt, by the feeling she was getting close.

Stephen finally tapped her on the shoulder, and she paused, blinking up at him.

"Did you find it?" he asked, rubbing his eyes with his thumb and forefinger.

"No, but I think I'm close," she said, trying to stay focused on him instead of rudely looking back at her holo and getting back to her search.

"Well, we're going to have to look for it later," he said, tucking his holo beneath his arm and holding his hand out for hers.

"But why? I'm close. I can do this. I need to do this," she said, her voice sounded too much like begging to her own ears and she swallowed down any other comments.

"Zellendine, if we go to our quarters now, we might get four hours of sleep and we have a lot we still need to look into tomorrow. Not to mention the influx we'll get."

The influx. She had forgotten about how busy they always were the first day after the transfer started. And they did need to look into the wombs as well as the tanks.

She rubbed a hand over her face and stood up, handing her dad her holo.

They walked down the hall and put the holos in their places in the clinic before heading to their quarters. No words passed between them and it felt like the secret of their crime was following them, stifling their voices.

Once they reached their living quarters, Stephen dropped

directly into his bed, but Zellendine wasn't ready to lay down yet.

She grabbed a snack from the service and sat at the table. Her mind didn't keep running through the issue of where to find the files, nor did she find herself thinking about the wombs or the people still sleeping in their tanks. Her mind was filled with the shattered window, with the terror of the moment she was sure she would die, and the look on Troylus's face as he remade the world.

Zellendine knew she needed sleep, so even though she was sure her dreams would fill with that moment and she wasn't entirely sure if she would fall asleep at all, after her snack was done, she laid in her bed and shut her eyes. But the image of Troylus, bathed in his own blue light, was painted on the back of her eyelids.

TROYLUS

He didn't want to head to the starwalker office. Taking a day off, claiming to be sick crossed his mind, but if he wanted his crew members not to think about what happened and not to think about how a starwalk had changed the color of his eyes, he knew he had to act like it was just another day.

On the way to the office he passed the clinic, people were already waiting inside, but he stopped in the hall anyway. He wasn't sure what he was doing, he didn't really want to talk to Zellendine. He didn't want to fight with her, and he was so incensed whenever she was there lately, he didn't trust himself not to fight. But a part of him wanted to see her, needed to see her, even if it was just through a doorway.

Someone waiting moved and Zellendine appeared beyond them. One minute he was scanning the room and the next he was staring, unable to form a thought, let alone know what he should do. She looked up and made eye contact with him. She took a step in his direction and someone tapped her on the arm, stopping her in her tracks.

Zellendine smiled at him, a small smile that still seemed full of awe.

Anger flared inside him, but he managed to smile back, and she turned to the people waiting for her to help them. Troylus didn't know what it meant that the wrath where she was concerned wasn't gone. He couldn't figure out what it said that he had saved her life and was still so irrationally messed up when she was around, but he didn't like it. And it made him like himself less.

Somehow, he was going to have to get over his issues with her, because as he walked down the hall to the starwalker office, he wanted to see her again.

Through the office door he could see Maurice and his dad at the comms.

"Are they walking?" he asked, poking his head into the room.

"Troylus," Maurice said, jumping in his seat. "You startled me."

"Sorry," he mumbled. He wanted things to be normal, but Maurice was already on edge.

"Yes, Parmita is checking all the shields and the others are making a couple repairs," Rullon said before he tapped the ear piece and started rattling off information about the sealers and how much they had in stock.

"What repairs?" he asked, trying to be casual even though his hands had a white knuckle grip on the door frame.

"One of the windows for a cryo bay has seals that aren't right," Rullon said, immediately going back to explaining something to the other person on the comm.

Troylus's knees almost buckled beneath him. The seals on a cryo bay window... It had to be the one he put back together. He hadn't even thought to look at the seals around the edge of it.

"Are they lifting the shields?" Troylus asked, trying to keep his voice steady.

"Yes, some of them anyway," Maurice said, "Alara thinks keeping them all closed will frighten people."

Keeping them closed might save the Wheel, he thought. If that anomaly came back after what it threw at the ship before, Troylus didn't trust it not to attack again.

"I don't understand how that happened and it didn't have any effect on the cryo bay." Maurice shook his head and tapped something on the map in front of him.

Troylus took a deep breath and let go of the doorjamb. Maurice didn't seem to make the connection between his star-walk of the night before and the conundrum of the seal that didn't exist and didn't seem to be needed.

"So, do you need me to get on a suit?" Troylus asked, even though the last thing he felt like doing after the last time was starwalking. If he went out there again, he might explode in more blue light and fuse something together that shouldn't be.

"Not today." Rullon leaned back from the comm and stared at Troylus, twisting his mouth to the side and squinting his eyes. "Actually…"

It was never a good thing when Rullon said actually. Troylus braced for his dad's next words.

"Next shift's crew is getting their check up done in the clinic and I think you should stop by there to let them know they can come inspect their equipment here whenever they're ready." Rullon raised his eyebrows; he was terrible at being subtle.

"Okay, sure." There wasn't much else Troylus could say under the circumstances.

He nodded and walked away, his steps slow and dragging. His dad clearly wanted him to get checked out. Or, at least his eyes.

Rullon would probably find out if he hid in the orchard or

went back to bed, but he didn't want the anger to rise up again. And he especially didn't want to talk to Zellendine about the window or his eyes. He wanted to see her, but not as a medic while surrounded by people, and he didn't want to talk to her until he was sure he wouldn't say something mean for no reason.

An approaching contingent of crew from the next shift saved him from facing Zellendine. He relayed Rullon's message and went back with them to do their fittings.

The entire time they chatted about work and getting back into the swing of life outside of cryo, Troylus dreaded what he was going to have to do once he was finished helping them. He needed to go to the clinic and have his eyes checked, his dad was right that he should, and his dad expected him to get it done. Hopefully he could get Stephen as his medic. More than that, he did need to talk to Zellendine. And keep himself together while he did. He just wasn't sure how.

ZELLENDINE

"CAN YOU PULL UP THOSE TEST RESULTS ON THE HOLO?" Zellendine's dad asked, ducking into the office, bandages in his hands, on his way to wrap up the knuckles of an engineer who jammed them when he was trying to replace a panel in one of the living quarters.

"Sure, Stephen," she said, but he was already gone.

The first day after transfer started was always busy in the clinic, but at least they were almost done, and she was minutes away from meeting Briar back at the cryo bay. She hadn't slept much the night before, tossing and turning with her eyes firmly pressed shut, hoping for sleep until the chime over the ship's speakers announced it was time to start the day. And it was time for her and her dad to go to the clinic.

It was all she usually wanted to do during the day, be with Briar, but she had responsibilities, and no one on board ever shirked their duties.

At that moment, though, she knew Briar would have to wait until after she talked to Troylus. Thanked him at least. She had toyed with the idea of telling her dad she was sick, too tired from the night before, and then she could have gone to find Troylus or gone back to the cryo bay. The entire time it took her to get the clinic ready in the morning had been spent running through the possibilities of how it would work out, and how it wouldn't lock her into staying away from the cryo bay and being out of commission to help. Of course, she decided against it. It just wasn't something that was done. Breaking the law by looking backward was more than enough rebelling for her. Instead, she was in the clinic, doing check ups on the members of the incoming shift and helping the incoming medic crew get updated on what was going on.

Including the infant problem.

"So, whatever is happening, we can see exactly when it started on your shift and compare all the tests from that to any additional issues that pop up," Dean said, pointing to the log regarding the birth that looked for all the universe to be perfectly normal from the data.

"Well, yes," Zellendine said. "But we have to deal with what little information we have from this first case because we're only assuming it was a fluke and we did maintenance on the womb instead of running additional tests."

"It should have been a fluke, but now with the cryo issue..." Dean let his sentence die instead of finishing it.

The implications weren't lost on her either. They were still over one hundred years from their destination planet. If they couldn't rely on the wombs, and they couldn't rely on the cryo tanks, would there be anyone left to colonize the planet?

"Right after we're done here, I'm going back to the cryo bay to work on that problem too," she said, trying to get herself back on track.

Back to the place where these were just problems waiting for a solution, like all the other issues that popped up on board the ship. There had to be an answer, a way to keep moving forward for everyone else, even while she looked into the past.

Chimes rang out from the communication system.

"Are you all set here?" she asked, giving him the holo they were using and grabbing another.

Dean waved her away, engrossed in the data before him, chewing on the inside of his cheek and eyes intent.

At least it wasn't just her and her dad now, trying to figure out how the impossible had happened and fix it.

She walked from the clinic into the hall, and had to catch herself on the wall when the ship lurched and the engines rumbled. Her steps were less steady today than they had been. No matter whether she found the answers or not, tonight she had to sleep.

Briar and Troylus were walking along the corridor toward her, their heads bent together and Briar's hands flying in over sized gestures.

Briar saw her and ran to take her hand and kiss her on the cheek while Troylus was left behind to catch up.

"How was your first day back on shift?" Zellendine asked and offered a small nod to Troylus who gave her the smallest of smiles in return.

"It was fine. Troylus wanted to come help," Briar said.

Any other time it would have made perfect sense for Briar to leave the terraforming department, find Troylus at the star-walker office, and for all of them to meet up somewhere. But Zellendine was at a loss for how she was going to navigate having a conversation with Troylus about the blue light while Briar was around. Besides that, she didn't know what a star-walker could add to the effort of figuring out the tank malfunction. The cryo crisis was completely out of his area of study.

"Sure," Zellendine found herself saying. "The more hands, the better."

There were a hundred cryo bays on board the Wheel and the stasis crews made the rounds through dozens in a day so it was odd to ever run into someone when visiting a bay, least of all to find both of the crews, a total of fifty people, inside one at the same time.

Briar, Troylus, and Zellendine froze in the doorway to the now full looking room.

"Zellendine, I'm glad you're here," someone from the milling group of crew said. "Did you find anything last night?"

So, they had not solved the issue. A huge part of her had been holding on to the hope that when they returned to the cryo bay it would be to answers and Upton awake.

"No. I'm sorry," she said. "I wish we had figured it out. But I'm here to keep working on it."

"And we're here to help her," Briar said.

Or to be a giant distraction, Zellendine thought as Briar rubbed his thumb along her knuckles where he was holding her hand and Troylus looked at her under his lashes with his jaw clenched before his eyes darted away again.

Members of the stasis crew stopped their conversations and started tucking their holos under their arms. A few shook their heads or hung them as they filtered out of the room.

"That was a little demoralizing," Zellendine said. "I'm glad they have such faith that we'll figure this out tonight." She walked into the room and started her own data collecting from the tanks, and what, if anything they could tell her about changes to the people stuck asleep.

"What do you mean?" Briar asked, taking a seat next to his brother and trying to keep the smile on his face even though it was tremulous. "Apprentices from the terraforming and starwalking departments and an apprentice medic is a crack team, guaranteed to be the saviors of the day."

"I sure hope so," Journo said, coming into the bay, followed by most of the family members of the other sleepers.

The families checked on their loved ones, talked amongst each other, and left Zellendine alone as she scanned through the information for each of the people asleep and each of the tanks in the stack.

REM sleep still showed up on all of their scans, that was what she expected. But she didn't expect their sleep patterns to remain so consistent. In real sleep, people cycled through the phases, not always in the deep, dream inducing REM. But these people weren't cycling. They weren't even wavering. Their pattern wasn't a pattern, but a steady, unending line.

"Hey, have you figured out any clues from that thing?" Troylus asked, standing beside her and squinting over her shoulder at the holo.

"You're squinting, is your eye bothering you?" Zellendine asked, looking at the eye she could see from where she was and noticing with a start it was completely silver.

"No, my eyes just get tired from looking at holos so by the end of the day I squint, that isn't new." Troylus looked up at her and Zellendine could see the silver more clearly. The green was gone entirely from both of his eyes, they were now completely silver and almost lit from within.

"Is it…" Zellendine leaned forward to see closer.

"Spreading?" He laughed, low and humorless. "Yes, both of my eyes turned into this after…" His voice trailed off, but he didn't have to finish.

"Listen," Zellendine said. "I'm sorry I dismissed you about your eye. I didn't know what was going on."

"Don't worry about it. As it turns out, things have grown way bigger than my eye color. You were right about that." Troylus gave a flash of a smile and turned a worried look back to the families of the people in the tanks.

Troylus was right that so much was happening that Zellendine could barely keep up, but it was hard for her to make sense out of the wrath and panic of Troylus from only two days before to the man who had saved her life, and the person standing next to her.

Slowly, the families started to drift out of the room, heading to their dinners and the myriad things they needed to take care of for the lives they would be living for the next year in the first full day of being awake.

"Zelle, can you come here please?" Briar said after his family had left too and just she, Troylus, and Grandpa Kason, one the oldest people on board, and the Alara of the next shift, were left in the cryo bay.

"Of course," she said, walking to him and letting him wrap his arms around her and bury his face in her neck. She rubbed his back as he shuddered.

"Upton has to wake up." Briar's voice rumbled through her skin, more like a vibration she could understand than a sound.

"He will, Bri. I promise I'll figure it out."

2 4

———

TROYLUS

WATCHING BRIAR HOLD ONTO ZELLENDINE AS IF SHE WAS HIS tether on a starwalk, lodged a heavy mass inside of Troylus. The barely tempered rage that boiled inside him whenever Zellendine was around lately, turned. It spilled and bled through him, morphing as it did into something else. Some other feeling he couldn't name, but still left his nerves raw and made him clench his fists and take long blinks in the hopes that he wouldn't combust in blue light.

He wanted to talk to Zellendine, ask her what it looked like from the other side of the glass as he rebuilt the window. He needed to know what her medic training might yield by way of checking out his eyes and anything else to make sense out of the impossibility of the day before. But these people, sleeping for the all the universe as if they would wake in the next second, rested and ready to get to work, needed her more than he did. And he wouldn't dare risk talking about much with anyone else in the room. Still... it was almost a physical need building within him, to know what the hell was happening to him.... If he could.

"Troylus," Grandpa Kason said, interrupting his thoughts. "I'm glad you're here for Briar. Friends are important at times like these."

"I'm not sure what exactly I can offer him, but I'm glad to give it," Troylus answered. Grandpa Kason always sounded like he was the human embodiment of looking back and it made Troylus want to ask him endless questions. But as much as Troylus hated the prohibition of looking back, and felt like it meant simply having it invalidated all of his past, he couldn't bring himself to ask Grandpa Kason any of the many questions he was desperate to.

"My Elisa is my best friend. I'm glad you and yours are working to wake her up," Grandpa Kason said and clapped his hand onto Troylus's shoulder.

Troylus jumped at the contact, even though his uniform blocked it, and then schooled his features and dipped his head as the old man forced out a smile and made his way out of the cryo bay.

Elisa was asleep like the others, trapped in her cryo tank, waiting for Zellendine to free her. Troylus had managed not to let the sleeping people's reality make it into his mind with any of the weight it deserved. Grandpa Kason had changed all of that with a few words.

Suddenly he wasn't standing there to give moral support to Briar, not that he really had been before, nor was he in the bay to talk through the blue light with Zellendine, which was his real goal. No. He was there to see what, if anything, he could do to help.

Grandpa Kason deserved to have his partner Elisa with him, awake, and everyone else on board deserved to go into stasis and wake up without worrying if they would get stuck dreaming forever.

Zellendine and the rest of the medics were the best hope for all of them to find a way to get back to normal. Troylus knew that, and yet… his hands itched with the need to be involved, like somehow his body was telling him that he needed to be there, that he was important.

"Hey, Troylus," Briar said, walking his way and rubbing his eyes with the heels of both palms.

"Yeah?" Troylus asked, shaking his head a fraction to bring him back to the moment.

"Can you do me a favor and be here to help Zelle?" Briar asked, pulling his hands away from his eyes and blinking wide before a yawn took over his whole face.

Troylus's mouth crooked up in a smile, "First day, you're zonked."

Briar laughed when he was done yawning and nodded his head. The first day out of cryo always took a lot out of a person.

"Of course, I will," Troylus said and Briar flashed a smile at him although his eyelids looked heavy enough that he could fall asleep standing up.

"Thanks, don't let her get so lost in the hunt she forgets to eat alright?" Briar asked as he headed out the door.

Zellendine was already stuck in her holo, tapping away at it. She was so focused he doubted she noticed how unsteady Briar was and Troylus made a mental note to himself to look out for Briar asleep in the halls. He wasn't at all sure his friend was going to make it back to his living quarters before sleep took him.

He took a deep breath and stretched his hands at his sides, prepping himself to talk to Zellendine. He wanted to be helpful and keeping his irrational anger at bay was a requisite to that mission.

"Do you want me to go get us something to eat?" he asked, his voice came out too loud in the silent cryo bay and Zellendine snapped her head up to look at him.

"What?" she asked, her voice setting the rage alight inside him.

Apparently, he thought to himself, he wasn't loud enough. He tamped down the urge to yell at her and tried again.

"Briar asked me to make sure you eat, do you want me to get us something?" There, that wasn't so bad that time. He almost sounded nice to his own ears.

She smiled and nodded, "thank you. That would be great. And I would probably forget, if left to my own devices."

"Okay," he said, but he lingered, wanting to talk to her about the night before, but not sure how to form the words.

"Hey," she said, tucking her holo beneath one arm and making her way to his side.

The anger was there, but now it was easier for him to shove it to one side and focus on what she was saying.

"I..." she trailed off and Troylus waited, barely risking breathing and trying to keep the wrath firmly walled in just in case she called him a freak. "I wanted to thank you."

"Thank me?" Poof, in an instant, the anger was gone. For the first time since he woke up this shift, and didn't have a space anomaly trying to kill someone to deal with, the only thing he felt toward Zellendine was shock.

"Yes. You saved my life, Troylus," she said and the sound of her voice saying those words, that he saved her, made him think for a moment he would never be angry again.

"Well..." he said, not sure how to continue that sentence.

"Now, I don't know how you did it. And I'm not sure if I hallucinated what happened and it's actually something that makes sense to a starwalker, but, thank you."

Her voice was soft and Troylus couldn't help it, he wanted to confide in her that she wasn't wrong and had not been seeing things. He really had fixed the window with a blue light that poured out of him. But maybe it was better if she doubted.

ZELLENDINE

Troylus was acting like he was caught in the middle of a leadership meeting farting while naked. His mouth opened slightly and closed again without him finishing whatever he was about to say.

Zellendine thought about letting him stay that way and not pushing the matter, but her curiosity was building inside her until questions burst from her mouth.

"That really happened, right? Blue light poured out of you and you fixed the window." She glanced beyond his shoulder to stare at the window that looked like it had not taken a direct hit from whatever that thing was that materialized out of nothing.

"Um," he muttered and rubbed the back of his neck while he avoided eye contact until he dropped his hand and trained those strange eyes on her. "Yes. It happened, but I have no idea what the anomaly was, or how I did it."

"You've never done that before?" She realized she was using the same voice she spoke to her patients with and bit her bottom lip to stop from peppering him with a mass inundation of questions he likely couldn't answer.

He laughed. "No. I couldn't have even thought up doing something like that."

"So, what happened?" She tamped down the urge to start checking him out immediately and forced herself to stop wishing she could drag him to the clinic and run every test she could think of.

"Well," he started and through fits and starts he relayed everything, from the anomaly on the map, to the thing turning into a solid object as he watched, to the desperate feeling of needing to save her that resulted in the blue light and the repair.

He told her everything, but none if it made sense, still.

"Troylus, what does it mean?" she asked, her voice hushed and a level of reverence in it she heard although she wasn't sure it was possible to talk about this without it. She shook her head and tried not to let him know how much she wanted to protect him from the blue light, this friend of hers who, even when he had not been wanting to talk to her recently, still managed to perform some novel feat to save her life.

"Zellendine, I have no idea." He took a shuddering breath and gave her a wavering smile before he stepped past her toward the door.

"Where are you going?" she asked.

"You do still need to eat. We can figure out blue lights and anomalies after you find a way to wake everyone up." He flashed a more convincing smile at her and left.

Right. She had work to do. She couldn't let herself get distracted by Troylus, when he was right. They could figure out what was going on with him later, it wasn't a risk. Or, it didn't seem to be, it seemed like a positive development. But the tanks... they couldn't wait. At least they shouldn't anyway. The people in them and every member of her crew needed an answer before the month was out so they could be sure they wouldn't suffer the same problem with their tanks.

Zellendine tapped away at her holo and wondered, if she couldn't figure it out, would they all stay awake just in case, guaranteeing they never saw the planet they had been heading toward her entire life? Or, would all the people on her shift, including Troylus, try going into stasis anyway and hoping one of the other shifts could figure out the problem. And if they did make that choice, what was the possibility that it would prove fatal if the tanks malfunctioned further than they already had?

She tapped faster on her holo. The small of her back grew clammy with sweat as she still couldn't find her way into any sort of file that looked back and therefore would be helpful. All of the current data said the same things and told her nothing. The stasis crews couldn't make sense out of the readings and if anything was obviously wrong, they would have been able to, right?

Unless the leadership told them not to alarm anyone.

The errant thought stopped her hand mid tap, it hung in the air, her fingers bent in the aborted attempt to try another avenue to look for what she thought she needed to solve the puzzle.

No. The leadership wasn't hiding anything, least of all from her. She was working well with the stasis crews and one of those crews was on the same shift as the sleepers. No way.

Zellendine refocused and wondered if the series of problems, the womb, the sleepers, and the strange anomaly in space that seemed to have attacked her was making her paranoid. No, she didn't think it was that. She did think it was probably her own fear of being caught looking back manifesting. That made sense.

Maybe she should do a work up on herself for her brain chemistry and see if she needed medication to help with her paranoia. Not that it was ethical to do a work up on herself, but she definitely couldn't risk telling one of the other medics why she was growing paranoid. And she didn't want her father to tell her to stop looking backward.

Whether it was good for her mental health or not, she had to keep going, to find a solution. And after she did, maybe, she thought, she should look back to find a solution for the wombs too. Even if Alara had specifically denied that avenue of inquiry.

A shudder ran along her spine and her hands started to shake. Even with her complete belief in looking back to fix the tanks, the thought of breaking the law again to help the wombs triggered all her old concerns, it set off the alarms inside her head that had been reinforced daily by the motto of the ship.

Maybe the holos didn't actually hold any old files. Maybe it was for the best if they didn't. No. She didn't believe that.

With a start she realized that she truly did believe looking back was the only way.

The holo search proved just as frustrating as it had the night before. Somewhere the logs of things not saved to the current file had to be in the damn thing. She knew it.

Troylus came into the bay with two boxes from a server in his hands and sat down on the floor next to where she was before handing her a box.

"I promised I would make sure you eat, so sit down and eat."

Even though she wanted to keep going, she did as he asked. At some point she was going to hit the wall of tired and hungry at the same time, that likely wasn't good for her ability to figure out the holo.

"So, what exactly are you doing to try and figure this mess out?" Troylus asked, taking a big bite out of the bar in his hand.

Her mouth opened and shut with only a squeak coming out. He stopped chewing, his mouth pursed and his eyebrows knit together.

"You don't want to tell me?" he asked, his voice laced with

the kind of rage he had turned on her so often since they woke up this shift.

"I…" She mentally slapped herself. She had to get it together or he would know something was up, and the last thing she wanted to do was put Troylus at risk too. If she told him and he didn't relay the information, he was breaking the law too.

2 6

TROYLUS

HE WASN'T SURE HE UNDERSTOOD WHY ZELLENDINE LOOKED more pale than usual and was having trouble forming sentences, but he didn't like it. After spending the day pushing aside his anger at her, her obfuscation made it flare back with a vengeance.

"Fine," he said. "Don't tell me."

"No, Troylus," she said. "It's just, I'm not doing anything yet." She dropped her head into her hands.

Well, shit, he thought. He definitely made that worse.

"I'm sorry. You're trying to do something, I get that this is bizarre and no one knows what things they are supposed to do to figure it out. I was just trying to find a way I could help." His voice was shaky, but he kept it low and controlled enough that he thought the furious tone of it was hidden for the most part.

She looked up at him and he could see the dark circles under her eyes, heavy on her pale face, that told him she was actually as zonked as Briar was, but she was forcing herself to keep going. For these people, sleeping so deeply they weren't even aware of the stress she was putting herself under to save them, she was going to push herself as hard as she needed to.

Zellendine took a shuddering breath and another bite before she responded, her face taking on the general jovial aspect it always had, but now he could see through it better. He wondered how often he had been wrong about her. In their past, he often thought she was a vapid, unquestioning rule follower who he was only friends with out of default and good memories from childhood. Now, well, she was keeping her mouth shut about him and desperately trying to help people. He respected that.

"Don't worry, Troylus," she said when she was done eating and reaching for her holo again. "I'm sure with all of us thinking about this problem, one of us will find a solution." She stood up and approached the tanks again, her fingers a blur as they tapped on her holo at a frenetic pace his eyes could barely follow.

He took a last bite of his meal and swore he heard her mutter under her breath, "If I can just find a way in."

It didn't make sense to him. He sat on the floor and squinted at her, trying to puzzle out what she meant. He couldn't have imagined her saying that if he didn't know what it meant, right?

But then again, he had seen and done the impossible, adding hearing voices that weren't actually there wasn't exactly a star-walk with no tether.

Troylus did manage to be of help, when Zellendine asked him to grab another holo and check the vitals of the sleepers. Although he was positive it was busy work and had been done a thousand times already, he did what she asked and then he climbed the tanks to roll the sleepers from side to side and check for what Zellendine called bed sores.

"Bed sores develop when someone remains in one position

too long outside of stasis," Zellendine said, her eyes never leaving the holo and answering his unasked question.

"Have you seen that before?" he asked, his voice a grunt as he bent at an awkward angle to roll Grandma Elisa and check her as gently as possible.

"No, but it's in our training literature so we know not to let it happen when we have patients who need surgery or..." She trailed off and when he looked her way she was biting her bottom lip and staring at him, her eyes looked watery.

"Oh," he said, avoiding bringing up the accident that had taken both their mothers.

There were people who had made it, but had been in the clinic for weeks. Neither of their mothers ever made it to the clinic for bedsores to be a concern.

"Yeah," she said and rubbed at her eyes with her thumb and forefinger.

"Well," he said, hopping down from the tanks, done with his checks, "it's time for you to go to bed."

"No, I need to keep working, we don't have enough time for me not to keep working," she said, her voice picking up speed and shaking at the end of her pronouncement.

She focused again on her holo, tapping even faster than she had before although he wasn't sure how her fingers moved at that speed.

His anger flared back, and he leaned against the tanks to suppress it. No way was he going to let it derail this hunt for answers, and the best way he knew to help with the hunt was to get Zellendine to agree to sleep. He couldn't do that if he was screaming at her. No matter how amiable she usually tried to be, he didn't think she would appreciate an outburst from him, and he needed her to listen, not rage back.

"Zellendine, listen," he said.

She shook her head like she knew what he was going to try

to do.

He took a deep breath before going to her and putting his hand between her fingers and the holo.

"Damn it, Troylus," she said, her eyes flashing, before she spun the holo away from him and went back to tapping, her fingers slower and almost attacking the screen.

"No," he said, grabbing onto the edge of the holo and trying to yank it away from her.

"You need to let go," she said, her voice as rage filled as his own.

"And you need to get some sleep, or you're never going to find what you're looking for," he said, his voice a growl no matter how much he was trying to tamp down the flaring anger.

Zellendine opened her mouth to spit something else at him and then she froze with her mouth hanging open. Her hands let go of the holo, relinquishing it to him, and her head cocked to the side as she shut her mouth and smiled instead.

"What?" he asked, looking behind him because someone else had to have come into the room to get that kind of reaction out of her.

"Troylus, if this works, you're a damn genius." She threw her arms around his neck and hugged him tight, the holo, and his hands on it, pressing into his chest.

A tremor ran through him, from the top of his head down to his toes and all of his muscles tensed at once. Even his earlobes were cramping, and he was pretty sure there were no muscles in his earlobes.

She leaned her head back and was staring into his eyes, her face inches from his.

"Thanks, Troylus," she said and walked out of the cryo bay, leaving him holding her holo and unable to think of anything he said that could have been helpful. It wasn't genius to get some sleep, so what the hell was she talking about?

27

ZELLENDINE

SHE WAS MOVING SO FAST DOWN THE CORRIDOR, SHE HAD TO SNAG the edge of the doorway to the clinic to stop her momentum when she reached it.

Once she got inside, she went to the cupboard where the holos were kept and pulled out the blocky case she needed. It was rarely used, and she wasn't even sure she could remember exactly how to set it up. But that didn't matter, what mattered was what it was capable of.

Zellendine made her way back to the cryo bay at only a fraction slower a pace than the sprint she came down the corridor at, but she didn't need to grab a wall to stop her. Instead she careened into someone's chest.

"Holy shit, Zellendine, I thought you were going to bed." Troylus's voice sounded like he was either suppressing laughter or an angry scream, and she wasn't sure which.

"Oh, I'm sorry for running into you," she said, and checked that the case was undamaged.

Troylus stepped back from her and lifted his brow at the case in her hand.

"What is that thing?"

"It may be the answer to our problem, and," she paused to beam at him and link her arm with his at the elbow even though he stiffened in response she tugged him along with her toward the cryo bay before she continued, "I have you to thank for the inspiration."

"Yeah. I still don't have a clue how I inspired anything. Especially because you definitely aren't doing what I wanted you to." His face was turned more toward the wall than toward her and his voice sounded like he was clenching his teeth.

Whatever his strange anger at her was about, it clearly wasn't entirely gone, but she didn't care that much anymore. They were getting along well enough, and she was too happy to have a lead, any lead, to worry about his mood swings.

"No, I didn't go to bed, but I promise I will as soon as I am done with this little thing."

They reached the cryo bay and she let go of his arm to crouch down next to the tanks and open the case.

"So, are you going to tell me what this 'little thing' is?" he asked, leaning against the end of the tank and crossing his arms, his fists clenched.

Zellendine focused back on the case and tried to remember the exact details of how to do what she needed to with it.

"This is a machine that monitors the brain activity of someone while they sleep. It's more sensitive and specific than anything our regular censors or our holos can accomplish." She bit her bottom lip and squeezed her eyes shut, picturing the only time she had ever seen her father use the machine.

"How exactly is it supposed to help us, then?" he asked, his voice sad and full of… pity? Was he pitying her?

She rounded on him, ready to tell him where he could put his pity, but her brain popped up with the answers to exactly what she needed to do and she focused back on her task, talking as she did, forgetting entirely to be mad at him.

"I think if we track the brain activity of all of the sleepers here, over the course of the next four days, and then we track ourselves and Briar, maybe, if you're okay with that, then maybe we could see what the difference is," she said and bit down on her lip again as she attached the little censors to the places on Upton's head that they needed to be.

"And you think knowing the difference will tell you how to wake them up?" he asked, dropping his arms back to his sides.

His reaction didn't suggest to her that he held out a lot of hope of her plan working, but it was the best lead she had to go on.

"Yes, that's exactly what I hope will happen."

"Does that mean you're done searching until you get the data then?" he asked, rubbing his hand over his face.

"Thanks for that," she said, her voice a sneer as she finished the prep for the machine and pulled the mini holo from its side to turn it on and start the process.

"What?" He looked at her over his hand from where it hung in front of his face, his silver eyes glinting in the light of the room.

"You just reminded me that some people on this ship don't think I know what the hell I'm doing and that I care so little for my assigned duty that I shirk my responsibilities, so thanks for the reminder I did not need." She stopped entering the instructions into the machine and squeezed her eyes shut.

In no part of their journey had she let slip to anyone the feelings she had surrounding her job. Even Briar thought she was perfectly fine to be in the clinic. She never meant to tell Troylus about the pressure she felt under the circumstances, or to even for a second allow her own doubts about herself to be projected onto him.

A hand came down gently on her shoulder and her eyes flew open to see Troylus offer her a small smile.

"No one doubts either of those things, Zellendine. Just because I don't see how this could give us enough information to help the sleepers doesn't mean I think you're wrong." He took his hand off her shoulder and offered it to her to help her to her feet.

She tapped the last instruction into the machine and took his offered hand.

They walked quietly from the cryo bay and headed toward their cabins out into the corridor while Zellendine struggled to form the words to say what she wanted to.

"Did you want a different assignment? I know I did," Troylus said after a few steps, allowing her a chance to take a full breath.

"Yes. But I'm happy to be working with Stephen. And I'm going to keep looking, but now this gives me a chance to sleep too." She offered him a small smile and turned down the corridor toward her cabin and away from the way he needed to go.

2 8

TROYLUS

HE STOOD AT THE TURN IN THE CORRIDOR AND WATCHED Zellendine walk away, knowing her admission would remain in his head for days. The perfect child of the Wheel didn't always agree with the decisions made for them either. Troylus went to bed that night in his cabin, with Rullon snoring softly in the background, and tried to make sense out of her, failing every time he ran up against the things he had always believed to be true of the person he had known all his life.

When he woke to the chime over the intercom, Troylus didn't want to head to the tiny starwalker office. He wanted to go talk to Zellendine and Briar. He wanted to find out more about her and see if Briar was different than he had always thought too.

"If you want to stay here and keep sleeping until the second chime," Rullon said, taking a fresh uniform and a towel into the wet room, "that would be fine. Everyone knows you were up late helping the sleepers."

The door shut behind Rullon and Troylus climbed from the

bed to get some food from the server while he waited for his own chance to wash away the long hours of the day before.

Instead of refreshing him, getting ready for his day just made the million questions in his head louder.

Like, had Briar been placed in the assignment he wanted? Had anyone? Why were they placed in the positions they were? What exactly did the computer say about each of them to place them where they were? The Chapter computer system controlled so much of their lives, it even had a hand in which babies were born, picking which samples to be combined in the wombs...

The wombs.

His pace quickened; he had to catch Zellendine before she got too busy with the patients at the clinic. He had to tell her his suspicion.

Rullon stopped with his hand halfway to his mouth with a bar waiting to be bitten into when Troylus barreled through the wet room door, pulling his uniform on all the way and then darting out the door into the corridor without a word.

Troylus was still buttoning his uniform and rolling up the sleeves as he ran down the hallway, dodging around people he encountered along the way, not bothering to explain himself.

By the time he reached the clinic there were already people milling about inside and he wanted to scream at them all to come back tomorrow for their check ups, this was more important.

Instead of doing that, and earning himself reprisal from leadership for interfering with other people's jobs, he walked in calm and sure, past all the waiting people like he had a reason to be there.

Coming out of a side room, her arms full of a box some kind of supplies, Zellendine almost knocked him over.

"Troylus," she said, her eyes wide as she fumbled to right the box and took a deep breath. "Are you okay?"

"Yeah, I'm fine," he said, placing a steadying hand on the box and giving her space.

"Then," she said and paused, glancing around, "what are you doing here?"

He leaned in close to her ear, the anger in him increasing as he did, so he balled his fists up to control it and said, "I think I have a plan for the problem with the wombs."

She sucked in a breath and her mouth turned into a wide smile before she squeezed her lips shut and looked around them again.

"When you go on break to eat today, come get me," she said, flashed him another huge smile and turned away with her supplies.

Troylus wasn't sure what he had been expecting, her to drop everything she was doing and run with him to start on his plan, he supposed. But he had to admit to himself, through the fog of the anger he was sure was anything but warranted, that she had a point. They should both take care of their duties and work all the problems as they could. Otherwise they would both get in trouble with leadership.

He didn't mind that so much for himself, he thought as he walked out of the clinic and made his way toward the star-walker office at a much slower pace than before, but he didn't want to get Zellendine in trouble. Especially since he was starting to think she was the only person on the whole Wheel who was able to think the way they needed to. The only person who would be able to come up with the solutions to the problems they were currently dealing with.

Problems none of them had ever thought possible, let alone encountered before.

Besides, irrational anger at her presence or not, she was the only person he could talk to about the blue light, and maybe she would be able to find a solution for that too.

After they woke up the sleepers and fixed the womb problem, he was hoping they would have enough time before they went back into stasis for her to help him solve the mystery of him.

No matter how much he tried to push it away and pretend he was okay with it, he never wanted to have whatever happened happen again. He also really wanted his own eyes back. The silver still made him jump when he saw his reflection.

2 9

ZELLENDINE

HER FINGERS FUMBLED ANOTHER ENTRY INTO HER HOLO, FORCING her to delete it and start again. She had to focus, but the possibility that Troylus had figured out the womb problem along with the scans she was running on the sleepers made her brain run too erratically for her to be at her best.

"Zellendine, can you get the prescription for Anders?" Stephen asked, sticking his head out of the room he was speaking to Anders in.

Anders had diabetes, but she figured her father was spending more time checking on his mental health than going over his standard check up. Poor Anders must have been reeling from still dealing with the loss of his baby and helping his partner through all of her grief too.

She finished her entry into the holo and brought the prescription in to her father. Anders sat slumped in a chair, his hand linked with Yanna's.

He didn't look well, but it was Yanna's appearance that made Zellendine's steps falter.

The last time she had seen them, Yanna was wrecked with grief; now Anders looked more like she did at the time. Now, Yanna's skin was flushed, splotchy and it looked like she had hives. Her mouth was pressed shut in a grim line and she stared through Stephen, like he wasn't human at all, just something that held no meaning.

"Oh, thank you, Zellendine," Stephen said, making her shake her head and offer a wavering smile before she dropped off the prescription and hustled out of the room.

Looking at them, not knowing how to even begin to help them, it was too much for Zellendine and made her feel more inadequate than she normally did in her position. Part of the reason she didn't want to be a medic, all those years ago when she thought her opinion might matter, had been because she knew her father had to help lead people through grief.

Grief wasn't something she wanted to even think about, it was too close to thinking about her mother. And she was never going to be ready for that.

The best thing to Zellendine about the ship's edict to keep looking forward was that she didn't have to think about her loss.

So she shoved the sinking feeling of her gut into her feet and kept moving, continuing her work, hoping the chime would come soon and she could focus on the wombs with Troylus, focus on a problem that had a solution hidden within it somewhere.

At least, she hoped there was a solution.

The chime came and Zellendine shoved herself out the door of the clinic, her holo tucked under her arm before the sound even stopped.

Whatever idea Troylus had, she hoped it would work, if for no other reason than she never wanted to see another person with the same devastated look on their face that she just saw on Anders.

Her mother—the thought made her slow her pace for a second before she picked it back up again, she hardly ever thought about her mother, well, she tried to hardly think about her. And she never did in relation to grief, to loss. It was all too hard.

But when her mother died, she used the forward looking rule to pretend it didn't bother her, to keep going.

Even if it meant that every day she forgot a bit more about her mom.

Her brain couldn't hold the memories of the good moments at the same time that it denounced the pain of her loss and tried to forget it.

So, she forgot everything instead.

If they were able to fix the wombs, to ensure it never happened again, and maybe, just maybe, they were able to give a real answer to Yanna and Anders about why it happened, then maybe they wouldn't have to forget to move forward. And maybe they could grow to accept it and get back to a version of themselves closer to who they had been than the two people she had seen in the office.

Why were they meeting with her father? Did they blame her?

Zellendine wasn't sure what the answer to that was, and she wasn't sure she wanted to know.

In the hall outside the birthing room, Troylus paced back and forth, alone.

Briar wasn't with him, and she was surprised to find she was relieved by that fact. She wasn't sure if Briar would appreciate her spending any brain power on a problem other than waking up his brother.

"Hey," Troylus said, handing her the package from a service full of her meal.

"I forgot to think about getting any food, thank you," she said, and he flashed her a smile before looking up and down the hallway and ducking inside the room.

"Briar said you forget to eat." He opened his own package and took a bite before continuing. "So, I was thinking that about what you said the other day, about originally hoping for another assignment."

Zellendine's mouth dropped open and she pulled her head back like she had been slapped, but she was actually stunned.

"What in the universe does that have to do with the wombs?"

Troylus took another bite, nodding his head and smiling.

"I know why you say that, if I follow my own train of thought, where I landed to get my idea doesn't make that much sense to me either." He chuckled, low and soft to himself and it made her smile too. It had been too long since they could laugh together like they used to, and she realized that she missed it.

She realized that while she had been pretending all shift not to be upset by how coolly he had been treating her, she missed him. She missed her friend.

"Well, that's how ideas work, right?" she asked, smiling again, and taking her own bite.

He nodded and continued, "Okay, so I was thinking about the Chapter computers and how they decide so much for us, but they're often wrong."

Zellendine took another bite and stayed quiet, mulling over the heavy implications of what he was saying. She had second guessed the computers decisions, but she had never thought of them as being wrong before.

A feeling like the one she had when she thought about looking back made the bite of her meal turn to ash in her mouth.

"What I was wondering was, do the computers monitor the fetuses in the wombs? Do they have any control over the process once things are cooking in there?" he asked, his strange silver eyes somber, and his voice hushed.

"I…" Zellendine couldn't answer that. "I don't know."

30

TROYLUS

"How do you not know? Isn't that part of your job?" he asked, pushing the flare of anger back. This time he wasn't mad at her, he was livid that it seemed the computers had more control than he even realized.

Zellendine, as a medic, should have been able to answer that question. If she didn't know, who did?

"I…" She trailed off and wandered around the room, staring at the wombs, her face drawn and brow furrowed.

"When a couple want to have a child, we use their samples, or samples in storage the computer picks based on some parameters for health we don't have access to." Her voice was barely above a whisper and he found himself leaning toward her to hear every word.

"So, what happens once the fetus is growing?" he asked, bringing her back to his question, the one he thought more and more was the right one to be asking.

"Before this, I would have said nothing." She turned back to look at him, her face was edged in the panic he had seen on her only once before, the kind of all consuming panic that had taken over her entire body when the attack happened in the cryo bay.

He swallowed and crossed to her, slow so she wouldn't crack into the complete break down of before. He placed a hand on her shoulder and tried to put a reassuring smile on his face.

Maybe it worked, because she closed her eyes and took a shuddering breath before she leaned her head against his chest. He stiffened but stayed in place to give her time to think through all the things he'd been running over in his head all day.

"Troylus, what if the baby developed something at the DNA level that didn't fit the health terms of the computer? What if the computer killed the baby?" she whispered into his chest and he let out the breath he was holding.

"I was worried about the same thing." His voice was as quiet as hers.

Neither of them stepped back for a long few minutes, trying to cope with the possibility in their own ways while they leaned on each other for strength.

Zellendine looked up at him and took a deep breath before she said, "There's only one way to know, but I don't want you to get into trouble for it."

She seemed to be waiting for him to answer her, but he had no idea what she was talking about.

"You know I need to see where this goes," he said, "whether we get in trouble or not. This was my untethered decision, so I'm in with you. Whatever you have to do, you're not doing it alone." His hand was still on her shoulder, his thumb ran along her neck, venturing to touch her actual skin, her pulse raced. He wanted to reassure her, calm her, but he thought he might be doing the opposite.

"We need to look back," she said, almost without making a sound she whispered so softly.

"Look-" He cut himself off as his stomach dropped. He

couldn't bring himself to say the words aloud, he had thought them often enough, but when presented with the exact moment that he had to embrace the idea, the hair on his arms stood up and he lost the ability to speak.

"I know. It's… a lot, but it's what we have to do. I think it's the only way to be sure of what's going on." Her words were still barely audible, but she rushed through them like she had to get to the other side of saying them.

Once she was done talking, she slumped against him, his hand still on her shoulder felt her heartbeat flying through the vein in her neck. It matched his.

The same feeling he had whenever he used to do a starwalk was on him. Complete with the desperate need for more air. He sucked greedily for each breath and it didn't feel like enough.

"We don't know what they'll do if we get caught," he said, and she nodded her head against his chest.

"I know. But I don't know how else to accomplish this or the cryo tanks. I've been trying to look back in the holos for days."

"You have?" He pulled back from her and looked into her eyes, seeing his own fear mirrored in hers. But she also looked… resolved.

"Zellendine," he said, pausing and shaking his head while a smile broke out on his face.

"Of all the ways I thought you would respond, smiling wasn't on the list," she said, ducking her head and biting her lip to stop the smile tugging at the corners of her mouth.

"Well, I'm just proud of you, I guess," he said, and she shoved at him, her smile breaking into a laugh with a hysterical edge to it.

"No, I mean it, Zellendine." She stopped laughing and looked at him, her face falling back into the look of equal parts fear and resolve. "You're doing everything you can, I admire that."

She took a few deep breaths and straightened her shoulders, "So…"

He heard the question there, even though she didn't say it out loud.

"Yes. I'm in. I'll help however I can."

31

ZELLENDINE

"Okay, so how do I help?" Troylus asked, stepping back from her and looking around the room, his eyes hard and jaw set like he was preparing to fight the wombs.

"What I really want is some way to do what I need to. I've been tapping away at my holo for two days and haven't been able to find the way to look where I need to." She rubbed her hand over her face, the frustration she felt about her inability to find the way in weighing on her all over again.

"I don't know about the holo programs you use, but I can look back in the flag system for the starwalkers," he said, walking by one of the wombs and cocking his head to the side to look more closely at one of the tubes running out of the back of it.

Starwalkers could look back? What? She took a second to shake her head, her mind turning faster than the ship's rotation as she wondered if she could use his knowledge to find a way to look back in the files she needed to gain access to.

"How are you allowed to look back?" she asked, her voice hushed and tinged with anger.

"Oh, well, we need to constantly assess the trajectory of flags, other things in space, what not, and if their paths change, so we can anticipate them as much as possible before they become a problem for the ship. We have to." Troylus straightened up and turned to look at her, his mouth dropped open a fraction as it dawned on him what she was getting at.

"You think I can show you how we do it and repeat the process for the files you need," he said, his own voice hushed.

Zellendine nodded, and his eyes lit up. Beyond the strange glowing silver, his eyes shone with a wild glee while his smile grew to the point of being grim, and kind of scary.

"Nice villain impression," she said, laughing until she had to lean over and brace herself on the womb beside her.

"Villain?" he asked, rubbing his hands together and wiggling his eyebrows, "I like that idea. Now that's an assignment I can get behind."

"Troylus, you're making it worse," she said, laughing while she dropped to the floor, unable to stand anymore.

"After what we just talked about, I can't believe you can make me laugh," she said, closing her eyes and dropping her head back with a grin still on her face.

The noise of Troylus dropping down beside her made her open her eyes and look at him, the grin dropped from her face when she did, his face was drawn back to seriousness and he looked down at the floor instead of back at her.

"What's the matter?" she asked, sitting up straighter, her stomach flipped at the possibility that he might hand her another problem.

"Since we woke up this shift, I've been angry with you," he said.

For a beat she kept quiet, waiting for him to continue, when he didn't, she said, "I know." Hoping that maybe he was just waiting for an acknowledgement, because she didn't know what else to say.

"You need to know that it wasn't you. I can't even explain it. I knew as I was raging at you and avoiding you, and that it wasn't anything you did, and even that I wasn't being fair. But even when I knew it was irrational, I couldn't stop it. It would flair up whenever you were around. I can't pretend it's entirely gone, but I want you to know I'm trying and I'm sorry," he said, looking at her out of the corner of his strange eyes.

Zellendine took a breath and relaxed to leaning against his side. He stiffened for a second and then leaned back into her. She wasn't sure how to explain it to him, that she didn't care anymore. They had figured out how to be friends again and he was helping her. That's what mattered.

"Maybe the blue light doesn't like me," she said, smiling to herself.

"I…" He trailed off and turned to look at her. "Maybe."

He smiled and it softened the blow.

"It did save me though, so…" She let her own voice trail off and his smile grew.

"Well, that was probably a fluke, so maybe no more wars with invisible flags, yeah?" he said, laughing when she bumped his shoulder with hers.

"So, when can you show me how to access the starwalker computers?" she asked, focusing back on how they were going address their real problems.

Troylus's face fell back into his serious expression and his brow furrowed while he bit on the corner of his bottom lip.

"Well, that could be a challenge. We'll have to wait until the middle of the night and hope I can talk the night monitor guys into taking a break. The office is too small for me to surreptitiously access anything without them noticing. Especially if you're there." His voice was resigned, but his foot tapped against the floor and his hand gripped his knee where it was drawn up toward his chest.

She reached out and placed her hand on his, over his knee.

"It's okay. We'll figure out a way," she said.

"We have to," he agreed. "After I'm done today, I'll meet you back at the cryo bay and I'll have a better idea of when I can make it work."

"As long as we get it figured out before we need to go into stasis and before someone else uses the wombs," she said.

"Oh, shit." He clamored up from his sitting position, holding a hand out to her to pull her up as well.

"Um, what, oh shit?" she asked.

Troylus pulled her along by her hand to the hallway, only letting go once he was sure she was following him.

"I have an idea, but, um," he said, stopping to look at her. He grimaced before he picked up his pace down the hall again.

"Do you trust me?" he asked.

"Of course, why?" she asked. Although it was normally true, as she said it at that moment, she wasn't completely sure she did. Whatever his plan was, it didn't sound like he thought she was going to be happy about it.

They came around a bend and the starwalker office with the air lock and entry bay next to it came into view.

Rullon, Troylus's dad was in the office talking to a couple starwalkers from the next shift who Zellendine didn't know very well.

"I'm sorry about this," Troylus said under his breath, taking her hand. "Just play along, okay?"

She wasn't sure what he meant, but if this plan got them access to the computer, she was going to play along. Even if she wasn't sure what the game was.

32

TROYLUS

PART OF HIM FELT BAD FOR NOT TELLING ZELLENDINE WHAT HIS play was, but there wasn't time. He had hoped he would run into the guys from the night crew and talk them into letting him have some time in the office, but his dad wasn't part of that plan.

The night guys always stopped by during the midday meal to check the lists, the schedules, flags, and what, if anything, had been picked up by the day crew from where they left off. It was routine, and usually didn't mean a member of the day crew would be there, let alone Rullon.

Rullon had been spending more time than normal in the office, Troylus made a mental note to keep an eye on that. It wasn't lost on him that his dad might have been trying to find the anomaly again, or come up with an explanation better than the feeble one he had offered for his strange starwalk. But now, Troylus had to focus on a way to get Rullon not to ask questions about what he was asking of the night crew.

"Oh, hey, Troylus, Zellendine," Rullon said as Troylus pretended to pull up short in the doorway to the office, dragging Zellendine in behind him. Rullon looked to both of them, tipping his head to Zellendine before his eyes dropped to their hands together and his eyebrows flew up. They may as well have announced their intention to become partnered by being seen touching.

"Hey, I, uh…" Troylus stammered, looking anywhere but at the men in the room. "We didn't realize this room would be occupied."

Zellendine sucked in a breath behind him, her fingernails digging into his hand, and he begged her in his mind to forgive him.

She leaned closer to his side and he had to stop himself from breathing out a relieved sigh.

One of the guys from the night crew was a notorious asshole and he elbowed Rullon in the shoulder, smiling.

"You two can come back tonight when we're taking a meal break," the asshole said, leering at them.

"Great, thanks," Troylus said, trying not to sneer.

He turned and made eye contact with Zellendine who lifted an eyebrow at him and stomped off, still not letting up the death grip on his hand. He was sure his hand would have bloody little crescent moons from where she was digging her nails into him.

She didn't say a word until they were far enough down the hall that they wouldn't be heard from the office, then she grabbed him and pulled him into her against the wall of the corridor. She spoke into his ear.

"I'm sure this looks great from where they are, but you need to know that I would rather punch you in the throat than be this close to you right now," she whispered in his ear, her fists balled into the fabric of the front of his uniform.

"Zellendine, I'm sorry, I wasn't expecting my dad to be there and I thought just showing up with you would be enough for the asshole to assume, I didn't think I would need to lay it on so thick. I'm sorry," he said, trying to calm the racing of his heart and swallow beyond the dryness of his throat. All the anger at her was gone and it was being replaced by thoughts that would definitely piss her off more. She had to let go of him. His hands were braced against the wall on either side of her, he balled them into fists and doubled his efforts to focus.

"Fine," Zellendine said, shoving him away from her and releasing her grip on his uniform. "But if this becomes some rumor and Briar is hurt by it, that's on you. You get to explain it to him."

She turned, grabbing his hand, and dragging him after her. At least this time she didn't have her nails digging into his skin.

As soon as they were around the bend enough that none of the guys in the office could see them, Zellendine let go of his hand. He wished she hadn't, but tamped that down in favor of a list of all the things they knew and didn't know about the many dangers they faced. Something to focus on other than her, anything to focus on other than her.

33

ZELLENDINE

DAMN HIM, SHE THOUGHT. HER BRAIN COULDN'T HOLD ONTO anything other than her anger at Troylus. Who did he think he was? He turned her into the butt of a joke with the asshole in the starwalker office. Well, screw him.

She had thought he understood her enough to know better than to make her the butt of a joke.

"I guess not," she mumbled to herself as she entered an update to the list of supplies she needed from the supply crew.

"What, Zellendine?" Stephen asked, making her jump.

"Nothing." She was going to have to remember to keep her musings to herself, her dad was already at jeopardy when it came to what she was doing, just by knowing.

"Just talking out loud to myself, trying to keep too many things going in my brain at once, I guess."

"About that, um, project," he said, leaving off his actual question. She already knew anyway.

"There are tests ongoing, and I have a lead that I'm running down," she said, leaving her own answer just as vague in case any other medics overheard.

"Good. I'm keeping leadership up to date on any progress we make in figuring it out." His voice was heavy with warning. She hoped the guilt of not telling them everything wouldn't weigh on him too much. "I'm looking up all the information I can find on the problem. If you find anything, let me know, and I'll keep you in the loop if I find anything I think is helpful." Stephen continued his tapping on his holo, looking on the outside for all the universe at ease with the subject of breaking the law.

Even to Zellendine, he looked relaxed enough to be talking about what they were going to eat that night.

Well done, Dad, she thought to herself, wondering if she would ever be quite as good at faking it.

Maybe that was why Troylus hadn't warned her about his plan before hand. No, she wouldn't give him a pass on his shit. She was going to stay mad about it and he was going to have to earn her forgiveness.

Part of her wondered if anyone would even hear about it. People often found time to be alone with each other, partnered or not, it wasn't a big deal as long as no one saw. Although the possibility of Briar being hurt by it pissed her off, the bigger problem for her was that the guys in the office might make jokes about her. That she had a real problem with.

She mistyped in her holo again, went back and corrected her mistake and closed her eyes, rubbing her hand over her face.

It was going to be a long night, she still had to switch the monitor to a new sleeper and then go with Troylus, although she didn't want to, to go through the starwalker computer.

The chime came over the speaker and she entered the last of her order into the holo, idly wishing it was as simple as that for everything. It would be nice to order up an answer on how to get the sleepers awake and protect everyone on board from having the same problem.

Maybe she would get lucky and the sleepers would be

awake. She smiled and shook her head that she could still hope for ridiculous things in the midst of all the problems. Even if they did, she was going to have to try and figure out why it happened in the first place, otherwise how would she ever climb into a tank to put herself into stasis, let alone allow all the other people on her shift to do the same?

Instead of stomping down the hall like she did earlier in the day, instead of running like she did the night before, Zellendine wandered down the hall toward the cryo bay. The weight of the responsibility she had taken on making her feet drag and her shoulders slump.

At least her dad was looking for answers too. On his own path, yes, but at least she wasn't the only medic trying to find a solution. Troylus and Briar were enthusiastic, and Troylus seemed to have good insights, but neither of them knew their way around the problems in front of them. Neither of them could even understand what they were looking at when she looked at the scans on the sleepers. Neither of them could tell at a glance if the sleepers were healthy or not, if they were actually sleeping or not.

Sometimes she thought it was too much. She was twenty years old, not technically done with her apprenticeship until the next time she came out of stasis. How had all of it landed on her?

"Hey," Troylus said, his voice soft, breaking into her thoughts. He stood in the hallway in front of her, his hands tucked into the pockets of his uniform, his shoulders slumped, his silver eyes shining at her from under his lashes.

"Hi," she said, not able to come up with any other words and feeling the weight on her increase with every second they faced each other.

"Before we go to the cryo bay, I just wanted to apologize

again, for invading your space earlier. That wasn't okay," he said, shuffling in place.

"Troylus." Her voice came out in a whoosh of breath. He didn't get it. "I don't care that you held my hand. We're friends. I care that you made me the butt of the joke of the asshole on your crew." She rubbed a hand over her face until he touched her other one, a tentative, barely there, tap.

"Sorry," he said. His voice was sure, and he didn't try to explain it all away.

Maybe he did get it. Whatever the complications of his play, she had to admit that it seemed to have worked. But…

"What about Briar, though?" she asked.

He pulled his head up to look fully at her, his contrition seeming to be forgotten and replaced by uncertainty.

"I, um, if Briar finds out, I'll come up with something so any hurt he feels doesn't land on you," he stammered, closing his mouth again.

"That's not even what I mean," Zellendine said. "What about Briar right now? You know as well as I do that he won't want to be sidelined away from the search for answers."

"He – uh, you're right. But I'm not sure how to get around him."

"Don't worry, Troylus. I'll figure this part out. Your ideas are good, but your execution sucks." She bumped him with her shoulder as she passed him, continuing to trudge down the hall, but she was rewarded by his low laugh as he turned to join her.

TROYLUS

HE HAD TO ADMIT, ZELLENDINE KEPT SURPRISING HIM, EVEN though he was trying not to underestimate her anymore.

But as much as he thought she was right, and she would have a better chance of getting Briar to let them look things up alone, he had zero ability to imagine how she was going to convince him. It was his brother who was locked asleep after all, and his soon to be partner who was leading the charge to figure it out and save the sleepers.

Even the night before when Briar had been completely exhausted by his first day out of stasis, he hadn't wanted to leave his brother. None of the others had wanted to leave their loved ones either, but they all recognized how little their assignments could help. Briar didn't. He seemed to think that he had to be part of the solution.

Maybe Briar underestimated Zellendine too. Troylus couldn't believe Briar could know her as well as he must to want to become partners without realizing that she was more than capable. Troylus was just her friend and he had figured it out, but then again… he didn't know that until this shift, until this mess of problems, maybe it was the same for Briar.

Entering the cryo bay was the same kind of surreal experience from the day before. There were more people than was usual, some milling about, some talking to their loved one, sleeping beyond the reach of their words, and some were commiserating with each other.

"Zellendine, Troylus," Briar called from across the room, waving an arm their way.

"Here we go," Troylus muttered, Zellendine started walking toward Briar, her shoulders even more hunched than when he found her in the hallway. Whatever her play was going to be in order to keep Briar out of their looking back, she must have already been putting it in place.

Troylus managed to keep himself from shaking his head and smiling at her. That probably wasn't part of her plan, so he bit his lip to stop himself.

"Hey, what happened last night? Any news?" Briar asked, giving Zellendine a perfunctory kiss and sliding his arm around her back, his eyes moving from her to Troylus, wide with a fervor about him.

For the first time, Troylus found his anger flaring up at Briar, nothing toward Zellendine, but at his friend. He didn't even hear the first things they said to each other he was so far inside himself trying to figure out why he was mad at Briar for no reason. Was it just a replay of the irrational rage only with a new target? Why was it happening to him again?

"Actually," Zellendine said, her voice breathy and low, "it took all night, but Troylus said something that made me think up a plan. But it's going to take days until I know whether it will work or not."

Briar and the others around him deflated with her words,

making Troylus aware of how silent everyone had fallen. That kind of pressure wasn't going to help Zellendine, he thought. It wouldn't have helped him if he was in her position and he already knew she worried what people thought about her abilities.

He coughed, to draw some of the attention off of her.

"To be honest," he said into the silence, "I didn't do much, I was just support staff. Zellendine is doing a great job looking at all the angles while Stephen does research. I'm sure her plan will yield results."

She looked up at him, her eyes softening, and though she didn't say it, he could feel her thanking him.

"Oh, so what's the plan for now, then?" Briar asked, looking back and forth between Troylus and Zellendine.

"I need to look at all the data I collected from the special scan I did on Upton and move the scanner to another person sleeping. It will take some time, but at least maybe it will give me a chance to sleep." Zellendine's voice grew weaker as she spoke, she didn't take a breath until she was done, and even that sounded painful and strained.

Troylus had to cover his mouth with a hand, crossing his arms over his chest, and bite his lip to keep from smiling. She was brilliant.

All of the sudden the people around her started to clear out, many nodding to her with sympathetic looks on their faces as they filed out of the room.

"Come on, Briar," Journo said, tapping Briar's elbow as he passed toward the door. "There's nothing more you can do here, Zellendine needs to get done and get some rest. Besides, your sister missed you last night and she needs you more than anyone else does right now."

Journo and his partner waited at the door to the hall for

Briar to give Zellendine a hug and follow after them, looking over his shoulder to where she stood next to Troylus.

She trudged toward the stack of sleepers, and Briar left with his dads.

Troylus held it in, his lip starting to hurt from his bite, until he was sure all the family members were far enough away from the cryo bay that they wouldn't hear him, then he bent over laughing.

"Stop it," Zellendine said from where she was working with the things attached to Upton. But there was laughter in her voice and it just made Troylus laugh harder.

"You — " Troylus struggled to get himself under control and tried again after he stood and walked to where she was to lean against the stack of tanks. "You were amazing. I don't know what that skill is, but I never want to be on the other side of you when you feel like manipulating someone, damn."

"I don't feel good about manipulating anyone, but I had to do it." Her voice was equal parts acidic and sad.

"Damn it, I'm sorry, again. I don't mean it bad," he said, crouching down next to her so he could look her in the eye without her having to crane her neck back to look at him.

"Troylus," she said, her voice a sigh as she tilted her head to look at him, "I know you didn't. I'm sorry, that just sucked. I don't like keeping things from Briar, but I don't want you to know what I'm doing either, that way neither of you can get in trouble if I get caught. It's just a lot."

He watched her as she worked, disconnecting Upton and reconnecting the device to the person in the tank above him. As he watched, it dawned on him. Why he had been angry with Briar. He was jealous. He didn't have someone in his life the way Briar did. Someone willing to help him, even if it meant breaking the law. Someone he could casually touch in front of people without breaking protocols. Someone.

Zellendine finished up and stood over him, looking down at him with a smile on her face.

"What?" he asked, himself needing to tilt his head back to look her in the eye.

"Get up. I finally get to put you to work."

35

ZELLENDINE

TROYLUS WAS GRINNING AS HE MOVED THE SLEEPERS IN THE UPPER tanks and Zellendine did the same for the ones in the bottom. They still had time to kill before they would be able to get into the starwalker computers and she was wondering if it wouldn't be better if they each went to their quarters to steal a few hours of sleep, but she felt comfortable that they had a lead for the first time in days and her lie to Briar grew more fictitious as she worked, not less.

She wasn't tired. She was energized and couldn't wait to get to work on the computers.

"We should get some food and go do something while we wait," she said, surprising herself that she didn't suggest the sleeping option.

"Okay," Troylus said, dropping down from the top tank, landing right next to her, his silver eyes shining and a grin on his face.

"How about the orchard?" he said.

"Perfect, let me just check the read out from the scan on Upton real quick." She grabbed the mini holo and connected it to her regular one, not waiting until the transfer of information was complete before checking on what she had.

"Hmmm," she said, chewing on her lip and tapping away at her holo, bringing up another section of the information.

"I never liked that sound. Usually when someone makes it, I'm about to get in trouble for something," he said, leaning over her shoulder to look at the holo. His breath was hot on her neck and the tiny hairs it touched rose with each of his exhalations.

"You don't even know what you're looking at," she said, turning to face him leaving only inches separating them.

"Nope. But I thought it couldn't hurt to look." His grin was sly and reminded her of the times their instructors had made the same hmmm noise at him when they were growing up, before they got their assignments.

"Actually, now that I think about it, you did get into a lot of trouble when we were young," she said, laughing when he pulled away from her and put his hand to his heart while he wore a hurt expression.

"Well," he said, bumping her shoulder with his, "that just makes me the perfect accomplice. Come on, let's head to the orchard."

She finished up what she could do for the sleepers and tucked her holo under her arm before she nodded at him and followed him out of the cryo bay.

They found their way to some food, and Zellendine couldn't help but think about what she had said to Troylus in the cryo bay. Yes, there was a part of her that still struggled with the fact that Troylus was at risk simply by knowing what she was doing, let alone by helping her accomplish it. But another part of her, a part that watered the sprout of guilt in her gut, was happy she had someone she could talk to about it other than her dad.

"Maybe someday we should tell Briar exactly how good a

friend you are to him," she said as they turned the corner through the doorway to the orchard.

"What do you mean?" he asked, his brows drawn together as he veered off the path and started weaving through the trees.

"Briar doesn't know what you're willing to do. To risk," she said, her voice low and careful as she picked her words carefully, "in order to save his brother. I think someday he should know how great a friend he has. And I'm glad you're my friend too."

Troylus stopped walking and turned to look at her, his face inscrutable.

She bit her lip, wondering if she had said the wrong thing somehow. The whole universe felt like it was teetering with every breath and waiting to topple one way or the other, and in that moment, waiting for Troylus to respond, her heart pounded, and heat started to build at the nape of her neck, causing beads of sweat to threaten dripping down to the collar of her uniform. It was almost worse than waiting for him to respond to the truth about what she was doing for answers, waiting for him to respond to the truth about how much she appreciated him.

His finger brushed her cheek, making her suck in her breath and stop chewing on her lip, as he reached out and pushed a wayward bit of hair behind her ear.

"Zellendine," his voice was a cool wash over her fevered skin, a calming balm that slowed her heart and relaxed her muscles, "what he really needs to know is how lucky he is."

Troylus turned and kept walking, disappearing around a tree trunk, while she reminded herself that Briar could never know what either of them were doing. Even for Upton, she wasn't sure he would approve. She wasn't even sure he wouldn't turn them in himself.

36

TROYLUS

He had to shake it off. He had to shake her off. He knew that. Damn it. He knew. But holy shit, he didn't want to. He wanted to get further stuck into what she was doing, she was addicting to be around.

For years he had thought of her as his pleasant, but bland friend. But this girl, this take on too much, manage to get what she needs no matter what, willing to break the law, girl, she was more than pleasant. And he had to remind himself it didn't matter. His distraction didn't matter, their friendship didn't even matter, helping her figure this out to save them all, that's what mattered.

Troylus finally found his spot beneath the same tree he had visited with his sister under.

He smiled at her approach and she smiled back, some of the tension was gone from her face at least.

"Okay," he said, clearing his throat and grinning, "after we figure out the sleepers, I would like to help with the womb issue if I can. So, what else can I do?"

Zellendine shook her head, but she was smiling at him.

"I'm sure there's something," he said, leaning toward her.

"One crisis at a time," she said, waving her hand in the slow down motion they had received so often as kids running through the halls.

"You know, you keep waving your hand like that I'm going to have to start calling you Maddie."

She laughed and swatted at him.

"I am not like our teacher." But she stopped waving her hand around.

"When we get there, I'll let you know what all I'll need. Right now, I'm not even sure what I'll find or if there's anything there for me to discover. It seems like there should be an answer, but what if there isn't? And what if there is, but I just can't find it no matter how hard I look?" She took a bite of her food and stared out across the orchard, lost into the void of thought he could only guess at.

"Do you think it's happened often?" he asked, putting to words the question that had been nagging at him since their discussion in the birthing room.

"That's just it. I don't know. And none of us would. It hasn't happened as far as I can remember on our shift, but would I remember if it had happened when we were kids?" She took a bite of her food and shook her head at the same time he did.

"Neither one of us were paying much attention to that until Briar's dads chose to have Upton," Troylus said and she turned her gaze to him.

"Right," she said. "So, not only do we have a limited number of births every shift anyway, we only have our memories to go off of in regards to guessing if this really is a strange occurrence or not. Maybe it has happened, but we don't remember, and no one will look back and talk about it. Maybe it's happened on all the shifts a few times. That's why I need to look at the data and try to figure it out."

She took a big bite out of her food and Troylus followed suit, running through the possibilities and trying to prepare himself for her finding statistics that would make it harder not to be angry that they couldn't look back and learn so they could stop things like the malfunctioning womb from happening again.

"Why do you think we even have that rule?" he asked, shaking his head and taking another bite.

"You could offer me my own planet and I still wouldn't be able to tell you a good reason for it. I assume that it has a lot more to do with the planet we came from and the people leaving it thinking the edict would offer everyone a fresh slate somehow, but it's a burden now and whatever their initial intention, it has gone way too far."

Troylus made eye contact with her, and he was positive, by the slight downturn to the corners of her mouth and the tightness in her eyes, that they were thinking about the same thing. Maybe if the edict wasn't a part of their lives, they would have more answers about what happened to their mothers. And maybe they would have been able to really mourn.

"I miss her, and I wish I could talk about her to my dad," he said.

"Me too," she said, reaching out a hand to place it over his.

He saw his own history, a history he wasn't supposed to think about, let alone acknowledge, mirrored on her face.

Turning his hand over to hang onto hers, it felt like she was his tether to this new world where he could look back, if even just in these moments, that he was finally allowed.

"Come on," he said, popping the last bite of his food into his mouth and tugging on her hand so she would stand.

"What are we doing? I don't think it's time yet," she said, but she got to her feet, taking another bite of her food while leaving her hand in his.

"It's not, but there's something I want you to see." He

squeezed her hand before he let go, turning to look around the area until he spotted the stool his sister had used, and walked over to grab it from the base of another tree.

"Of all the things I thought you would suggest I see, a stool somehow wasn't included in the list in my head." She quirked up one side of her mouth after taking the last bite of her food in a teasing grin and he laughed.

"Fair. Although, I would love to know what you did think I was going to show you, for now, climb up here." He gestured to the stool and her smile turned into an inquisitive frown, but she did as he suggested.

Troylus climbed up after her, so he was crowding her back, almost leaning on her, and he reached out his arm to point past her toward the nest.

"Look," he said, knowing when she sucked in a breath that she saw it.

"But they're too little, aren't they supposed to still be in with the caretakers? Does Indigo know about this?" she asked, her voice soft and reverent.

"Indigo showed me. She said the birds did it all on their own and the birds have been feeding them too. They don't know why, but they hope it means their natural instincts are returning because we're getting close to the planet. They didn't stop right away when we left our last planet either." He smiled at the nest and the tiny creatures inside, before he stepped down off the stool.

Zellendine followed, but her eyes didn't leave the nest, even when she reached the floor.

"Someday, they'll be in a real forest. I can't wait to see them there." Her voice still had that awed quality to it, and he wondered if he sounded the same way when his sister showed him. Probably.

"Do you think all of these things are connected somehow?"

he asked, realizing that he had never connected the dots before, but if the very reproductive patterns of the birds were responding to some stimulus they weren't aware of, maybe that was true of everything.

"In some ways that makes sense. But at the same time, how could this purely biological process be influenced as well as our mechanical versions of the biological process?" She shook her head.

But he wasn't sure, he thought maybe that was the real question they should be trying to figure out.

3 7

ZELLENDINE

They left the orchard, Troylus was quiet and his face had taken on the same aspect he had at the beginning of their shift when he was still angry at her all the time. It pissed her off.

"Hey," she said, turning in the hallway, grabbing his hand to turn him toward her, stopping him mid-step. "What's going on now?"

"What do you mean?" he asked, looking around like someone else was in the hallway with them. No one was, most of the crews of both shifts were asleep.

"I mean, you look all brooding again, and it's irritating as shit." She crossed her arms over her chest and raised an eyebrow at him.

Troylus, eyes wide, snapped his gaze back to her and his whole face fell.

"Oh, crap. Will I ever stop needing to apologize? Sorry, Zellendine. I was just over thinking and lost in my head. I promise I wasn't lost in irrational fury at you again. Whatever was up with me at the beginning of this shift, it will never happen again." His face was so open, and he never broke eye contact.

His urgency to convince her that he was done being an ass, worked. She couldn't stay irritated with him. She dropped her arms to her sides, taking one of his hands in hers, and smiled at him.

"Okay, as long as it isn't that, you can go back to thinking too hard and brooding." She grinned at him and he laughed, shaking his head.

"Deal. Now how the hell are we going to do this next part?" he asked, turning and tugging her with him down the hall, not letting go of her hand.

"This is probably a good start," she said, squeezing his hand.

"Well, yeah. I just hope it's enough. I don't want you to punch me in the face." He grinned at her and she shook her head.

"I don't usually punch people, but I might slip some medicine into your next meal that will make you have to go to the wet room," she said.

He cut his gaze to her, his brow furrowed.

"You know I use the wet room all the time," he said, and she grinned.

"Not like this, you don't. I mean a lot. For an entire day." She laughed outright when he pulled his head back like she had punched him in the face.

"Gross, and mean. Damn, I underestimated your deviousness," he said, shaking his head.

Zellendine pulled her hand out of his and the laughter died in her throat. She was breaking the law, and about to break it in an irreversible, tangible way. Devious probably was the right term for what she had become, but it didn't mean she liked it.

"What? What did I do?" he asked, grabbing her hand and pulling her to a stop in the middle of the hall.

"Do you know how long I tried to be the perfect daughter of the Chapters? Do you know how big a deal this is for me? Devious isn't my natural state, and this isn't bad even if it is calculating. This is the only way. Of that, I'm sure." She shook her head and tried to tug her hand out of his grasp.

Troylus held on and wrapped his other hand around their clasped ones. His face didn't look remorseful, it was all hard edges and stark lines. He looked serious.

"Zellendine, you need to hear me when I say this. You are better than the perfect daughter of the Chapters. This version of you, where you do what needs to be done, Chapters and stupid ass edicts be damned, is my favorite version of you. If someone else has a problem with you, send them my way so I can explain it to them, and then kick their ass."

Somewhere in her chest something began to unravel. The tight ropes strangling her every minute of the day as she tried to maintain the façade started to loosen. She took a deep breath, full of lightness of truth.

"I am very lucky you are with me on this. Thank you," she said, her voice low and her hand relaxing in his.

Troylus looked down at their clasped hands, hunched his shoulders and tightened his jaw before he stood up straight, relaxing his muscles with a deep breath and a smile blooming on his face.

"Let's go, before you get mad at me again," he said and laughed, dancing away from her as she smacked his arm and grinned.

She started walking down the hall again and he caught up with her, his smile still in place to mirror hers.

He held his hand out, palm up.

Zellendine took it, threading her fingers through his, without hesitation.

38

TROYLUS

How much shit were they going to get from the guys of the other shift? That's all that was running through Troylus's head as the curve of the hallway gave way to a view of the star-walker office.

"Only two?" Zellendine asked, squinting toward the office.

"Looks like it," he said.

Inside were only two members of the other crew, the asshole not among them.

A chime sounded, the one for the lunch break for the second set of crew. Like the lunch chime for the other set of crew, it only sounded in the working areas.

"Where are they?" Troylus whispered and Zellendine gave him the tiniest of shrugs in response.

"Hey," Troylus said, once they were in the doorway to the office.

Zellendine took the chance to tuck herself into his side, behind his arm.

"I was wondering when you would get here." One of the guys said, rubbing his face while his partner pushed back from the holo panel and slumped in his chair. "We're down a couple for now, so do you mind if we have you stay for the whole meal? We really need a break. Flag that turned out to be ice or rock or some damn thing, tried to take off a chunk of us."

"Everything patched up?" Troylus asked, the hairs on his arms standing on end.

Zellendine stayed in the same position but he felt her body stiffen and her grip clamped down on his hand.

"Damndest thing," the other guys said, his hands still tangled in his hair as he stared blankly in front of himself. "Flag was coming right at us, saw it myself since I was out there shutting a shield."

Troylus nodded and wanted to reach out and shake the man, he wanted to scream at him to answer the question.

"But that flag was headed right at us and it just switched directions, flying off away from us like it had been hit, but nothing was out there at all." The man shook his head and dropped his hands, looking toward the man next to him and nodding.

Without turning his head, Troylus cut his gaze to Zellendine. Her eyebrows were high, and he couldn't make out if she was scared or angry.

Maybe he could have figured it out, but at that moment he couldn't puzzle out what he thought about it either.

"No problem, we can keep an eye on things for a while. Get yourselves something to eat and take a break." Troylus smiled at the guys as they walked out, nodding to Zellendine on their way.

Without a word, he and Zellendine both waited, barely moving, until the guys were around the bend in the hallway and couldn't see them.

"Do you think?" Zellendine asked, breaking the silence first, although her voice was barely above a whisper.

"That whatever the hell pushed that flag off track is the same thing that attacked before?" Troylus asked, slumping into a chair at the console and putting his head in his hands while he tried to control the frantic pace of his heart.

"You do." Zellendine dropped into the chair next to him, her shoulders slumped.

"But that doesn't make sense," Troylus said, throwing his hands wide and lifting his head to make eye contact with her.

She shook her head and shrugged, her mouth opening and then closing again.

"Why the hell did..." Troylus paused and ran his hands though his hair. "Whatever it is, attack and then defend the ship?"

Zellendine furrowed her brow and cocked her head to the side, looking him up and down and then staring into his eyes. No. Not into his eyes, at his eyes.

He pulled his head back and raised a brow at her.

"I'm sorry, Troylus," she said, shaking her head. "It makes no sense anyway."

She rubbed her eyes and gave him a wan smile.

"Nothing about this makes much sense, so try me."

"Well..." Zellendine bit her lower lip and looked around the room, her hands fidgeting in her lap, until she took a sighing breath and looked back at him, saying, "what if you're the key?"

Troylus burst into laughter, relaxing back in his seat and laughing so hard tears started to leak out the corners of his eyes.

"Fine. Forget I said anything. Just show me what I need to know." Zellendine shook her head and crossed her arms over her chest, turning to face the console.

"Come on, Zellendine, you have to admit, it sounds ridiculous because I am decidedly not that important," Troylus said, putting his hand on her shoulder and her stiffening at his touch.

"Your eyes are silver and blue stuff came out of you to

remake the window from shards of nothing. How is that decidedly unimportant?" She asked, whirling on him.

His laughter died in his throat, turning into a solid lump he tried to swallow around.

"Okay." He coughed, trying to clear the blockage in his throat that made his voice sound like a croak. "Let's say you're right. That this has something to do with me. What? What does it mean?"

Zellendine relaxed and took his hand.

"I don't know. But it just seems like that attack was some kind of test, and you passed. It disappeared after you pulled your trick with the blue light."

Troylus nodded, once, and ran his free hand through his hair, taking a deep breath and blowing out the air through pursed lips.

"We..." he started, and shook his head as a shiver ran through his body. Dropping Zellendine's hand and pulling himself closer to the console, he tried again. "We should get started, they'll be back eventually, and I don't want them to suspect anything."

"Sure," Zellendine said, turning to the console herself and pulling out her own holo, her focus seemed completely on their task.

Troylus tried to be as focused as he thought she was, he tried to forget what she had said. He really did try to pretend that she hadn't just connected his ability, the same one that had saved her life, to the most unnatural and bizarre things he had ever heard of.

While he walked her though the steps to look back on the computer for the starwalkers, and she followed along on her own holo, he tried to think that her connecting him to the anomaly didn't mean she thought he was as wrong as it was.

39

ZELLENDINE

Troylus went through the steps one at a time, waiting as she followed along with him, even when it took her awhile to find the right command in her own files.

"Shit. I did something wrong. Hang on, I'll go back," she said, trying to figure out which command would do what the star-walker file did.

"Maybe there's an extra step in yours that you have to take," Troylus said, his voice gruff and his eyes on her holo instead of her face.

"Hmm." Zellendine couldn't let herself wonder why he was so taciturn all of the sudden. She had to get this right on the holo. She had to.

After finding herself in a dead-end and backtracking again, Zellendine's heart beat picked up in pace. Her palms got clammy and the hairs on the back of her neck grew damp as heat flooded through her. There was only one option left. If it didn't work...

Zellendine paused with her finger hovering in the air, all she had to do was reach out. Just one tiny stretch. She tapped her holo. And that was it. She was in.

"I can't believe it. I started to think we would never get in."

"Wait," Troylus leaned over to look at the information displayed in front of her, pulling his hand back a second before he touched her arm and leaning back again with a nod to her holo. "Is that what you need?"

"Yeah," she said, slumping in her chair, a smile blooming on her face.

"Good." Troylus started the process of taking the starwalker computer back to where it was when the other crew left, while Zellendine tried to hide the fact that she was staring at him out of the corner of her eye.

What was his deal? She couldn't figure it out. One minute they were getting somewhere, and she thought they had made a possible breakthrough, and the next he was all weird. Not exactly hostile, like he had been before, but definitely weird and less than companionable.

Maybe he was just struggling to contain another round of irrational rage. Maybe he was just tired. She wasn't sure, but her own eyelids were growing heavier by the second.

"Now that I know my way in, I feel like I should just go to sleep in this chair," Zellendine said, with a yawn as an exclamation point.

"It's late. Go ahead to your quarters, I'll wait for those guys to come back." Troylus was back to resting his hands in his lap, but his gaze never left the console in front of him.

"Troylus, we're in this together. I'm not going to leave you to answer a bunch of questions and make it harder than it needs to be." Zellendine closed down her holo and touched his arm, he stiffened under her hand.

He turned toward her and took a deep breath before he opened his mouth to speak, but a thump behind her in the doorway made her turn around and he snapped his mouth closed again.

"Oh, I thought for sure we would have to be careful walking in here." The other shift crew members were back, their faces more awake with bars still in each of the men's hands.

"Very funny. I take my job seriously," Troylus shook his head as he stood, holding his hand out for Zellendine.

The men looked at each other and then stared as Troylus and Zellendine slipped between them and into the hallway, her hand in Troylus's.

Part of her wanted to turn around and make a face at the man who had a piece of his bar showing inside his gaping mouth. But she was exhausted, and she needed sleep if she was going to be able to go through the galaxies of information she could finally access on her holo. To say nothing of her hope to have enough brain power to figure out why Troylus was still acting like he expected someone to pop out from the walls and punch him in the face.

When they were past the curve in the hallway, Troylus tried to tug his hand free of hers. But Zellendine wouldn't let go.

She waited until he looked directly at her, his face the picture of exasperation.

Zellendine made eye contact with him, made a face with her tongue out, squeezed his hand and smiled before she let go. He only gave her one corner of his mouth turning up, but she took it and headed down the hall toward her bed.

40

TROYLUS

Waking up in his quarters, Troylus had a moment when he didn't remember the conversation of the night before. He had a blissful moment when he stretched and smiled to himself, his body still too tired from too little sleep, but relaxed and comfortable in the warmth of his bed. He had a moment to think only of how close they seemed to be to an answer, and of the orchard, of actually having fun with Zellendine.

But her name, the progress they made, all the flags hiding in his memories flooded back to him and left him too hot under his covers, and too cramped in his small bunk. The smile fell from his face and he opened his eyes on his empty quarters.

Rullon wasn't in his bunk, or anywhere else that he could tell from straining his ears.

He didn't know if he was supposed to be somewhere, likely on duty, but part of him didn't care. He had done his bit, played his role. Zellendine had enough information to continue the search and he wasn't much more help to her.

Troylus stared into the empty room and decided he had no more to offer the sleepers, Briar, or anyone else.

Soon they would go back into stasis and then they would arrive at their new planet, the only thing left for him to do was to starwalk and watch space.

Nothing had ever sounded less appealing.

Getting out of the bed was hard, getting ready was more difficult still, but walking through the hallways toward the starwalker office made his feet heavy. Each step felt like the gravity was increased, and his shoulders slumped, rounding on himself more the closer he got. Passing the clinic, he glanced inside and wasn't sure if he was happy he didn't see Zellendine or not.

Rullon was the only person in the office when Troylus leaned on the doorframe.

"Where is Maurice?" he asked, rubbing at a knot forming in the back of his neck.

Turning from the console to make eye contact with Troylus, Rullon crossed his arms over his chest and raised one eyebrow, leaning back in his seat.

"Maurice is with the others making some more seal and checking on our repair supplies. How much have you slept?" Rullon asked.

"Not enough," Troylus said and shrugged, dropping into the chair next to Rullon. He dropped his head back to stare, unseeing, at the ceiling.

"Is there something I should know?" Rullon's voice was patient and bland.

Somehow the very non-threatening nature of his dad's question and his voice as he said it, rang in Troylus's head like a warning of a trap waiting for him.

Part of him thought it would be easy to tell Rullon everything, to not be stuck with it rattling around inside his brain, running up against the same thoughts and the same doubts. Maybe if he told Rullon he would give him insights that could help him figure out how to walk away from Zellendine.

But another part of him knew that explaining everything to Rullon would put him at risk and he didn't want to test his dad's loyalty to him compared to the Chapter law.

Maybe, though, he could try and get some guidance without putting him at risk of keeping too many secrets.

"Zellendine and I are..." Troylus couldn't find a way to say what he needed to. He ground his teeth together and rubbed his hands across his face before he tried again.

"She... she's not what I thought. I mean, she's more than I thought." He laughed without humor. "But I don't think I can keep being friends with her and it sucks."

Troylus snuck a look to his dad who sat with his head cocked to the side and his jowls more pronounced, staring back at him.

"You don't know what to say either?" Troylus asked, a smile twitching his mouth before it disappeared again.

"I know what to say, I'm just trying to figure out if I should or not," Rullon said, turning back to the flag map, devoid of any signs of trouble.

Troylus sat up straight and waited for his dad's explanation. And he kept waiting. Finally, he shook his head and asked, "Okay, so are you going to tell me? Or just pretend you didn't say anything?"

Rullon turned back to face him, his jaw tight beneath his jowls.

"Fine. I want to know what the hell you're talking about, unless she and Briar have called their whole thing off, because I'm pretty sure that no matter how butthurt in love you are with her, your only option is to be friends. Or are you seriously considering not being friends with either of them?"

His mouth dropped open and he couldn't find anything to say so it hung there, open and waiting for words that didn't exist in his brain.

"I… I'm going back to bed. I don't feel that great," he said, standing and walking from the office, Rullon making no move to stop him.

Nearing the clinic, he slowed, his steps faltered, and he stopped altogether in the middle of the hall.

Stephen was talking to someone in the front area and, once again, he saw no sign of her blonde hair, or her dark eyes, just the vague resemblance of her in her dad.

Troylus resumed his trek back to bed and hoped that he could just avoid her for a bit, her and Briar. If he could avoid them until he went into stasis, he might never have to figure any of it out. He might never have to find out if Rullon was right and her words, her insinuation that he was as twisted as the anomaly, hurt so bad because he was falling for her. Maybe he could just avoid having to face that complication and then he wouldn't care as much when she partnered with Briar. Maybe he could even be assigned to a different spindle than they got assigned to for landing.

Big maybe, and for that moment, he just hoped he could avoid thinking about it for long enough to fall back to sleep.

41

ZELLENDINE

She hooked the special sleep scanner to the last of the sleepers and scrolled through the information that the night before had gained her on her holo.

Briar turned the sleepers in their tanks, his feet not far from her face as he climbed the stack. She stepped back so she wouldn't get inadvertently kicked in the face and sat in the little chair by Upton's head.

The families of the sleepers were all talking with her father, but she didn't hear a word they said. She was solely focused on looking through every last detail on the scan she had from the night before while she waited for a chance to look back through the files when no one was around.

Not that the information the scan had given her looked any different than the others had, but she still felt compelled to pay just as much attention to it as she had the others. And she wasn't sure what Stephen could possibly be telling the families since he hadn't found anything either.

Of all the people milling around, the only person she wanted to be there, wasn't. Troylus hadn't been around all day.

"Anything helpful in there?" Briar asked, at her side and peering down at the holo.

"Done?" she asked instead of answering and gestured toward the stack.

"Yep. It doesn't seem like it's that big of a thing, turning them. Do you really think it's important?"

She took a moment before she responded, she wanted to snap at him. But that wouldn't accomplish a thing. So, she took a breath and tapped away on her holo for a few more seconds.

"Briar, trust me it's important." She didn't bother to explain. If he didn't remember what it was like in the aftermath of the accident, she wasn't going to risk someone thinking she was looking back to it by bringing it up. She couldn't afford the risk, especially now.

"Okay. Hey, are you going to be able to spend some time with me tonight, or are you still exhausted?" he asked, running his hand along her cheek.

"I am still pretty wiped. With this in my head, I haven't been sleeping well, even when I do get the time. Since it's almost my turn to have this thing on my head, I need to convince my body to sleep or the test will be worthless," she said, biting her lip on the lie. She was free to spend some time with him if she wanted to. It would delay her search through the holo, but she was sure she was going to find the answer and what was one more day for the sleepers to stay out? But she didn't want to, she wanted to finish what she started and wake these people up.

"Don't make yourself sick worrying, that's all of our jobs." Briar waved a hand out toward the room full of the family members waiting on her to save their loved ones.

Zellendine wanted to roll her eyes at him. He actually thought reminding her how many people were relying on her would make her worry less? But she just smiled at him instead and went back to her holo and the comparison of her scans to the ones she already had.

The part of her that had believed she would find answers in the scans had shrunk so small it almost didn't exist, instead she grew more certain that she would find the answers by looking back, but she couldn't ignore the information. Just in case it yielded anything, and even if it didn't, she planned on using the scans as an excuse to explain how she figured it out once she found a way to wake them all up.

"I'll try and stay healthy, but that means I should probably take this and head to my quarters now," she said, standing and tucking the holo under her arm.

"Can I walk you there?" Briar offered her his hand and she took it, aware that he held her hand differently than Troylus did.

Troylus threaded their fingers together, Briar didn't. She wasn't sure why Troylus was on her mind so much, other than that she felt more alone with her search when he wasn't around. He was the one person who knew everything she was doing and was helping her to accomplish it all.

Maybe he thought she didn't need his help anymore now that she had the way in that she needed. But he was the only one she could have looked through the data with, he was the only one she could have talked to about whatever she found. He was the only one who knew what was really going on.

While the families still checked with Stephen daily, while her father covered for her and made excuses to them about the like-lihood of them finding a cure, she found herself more alone in the vast expanse of space around the ship than she had ever felt.

As she walked out of the room holding onto Briar's hand, she was only more aware of how much she still needed Troy-lus's help.

Having his support alone saved her so much stress and worry about getting caught.

But maybe that was the problem, maybe he felt too weighed down by helping her.

She snuck a glance at Briar, the smile on his face as he glanced back at her belied any doubts he held about her ability to save his brother, and the grip he had on her hand suggested he was none the wiser about her actions.

Would he stand next to her, let alone help her, if he knew she was breaking the law?

No matter how many times she asked herself the question, she was never sure. It made her miss Troylus even more.

4 2

———

TROYLUS

HE MANAGED TO AVOID EVERYONE FOR TWO DAYS. HE DIDN'T spend the entire time in bed, he went to the office and on starwalks, but whenever he wasn't on duty, he was in his bed. Not just in his quarters, but in his small bed, curled up and facing the wall.

"There's nothing I can do to get you to come with me?" Rullon asked, standing at the door with his hand on the knob.

"No thanks, I'll see Indigo another time and there's plenty of food in the service now." The one outing he had done on his way back from the office was to get food because he was spending so much time in bed and he did still need to eat.

"Indigo is going to kick your ass if you make a habit of this, and I'm going to let her, just so you know," Rullon said, stepping out the door. It clicked shut behind him and left the silence around Troylus complete.

He turned his face into his pillow and squeezed his eyes shut, begging for sleep to take him away before the guilt and doubt could set in.

A knock sounded on the door, Troylus opened his eyes and

tried to figure out if he was dreaming or not. But it happened again, louder the second time.

"What now?" Troylus mumbled, dragging himself from the bed and rubbing his eyes. If Indigo was on the other side of the door, he was about to get reamed. But Rullon hadn't been gone long enough for him to get to her and for her to get all the way back to their quarters, had he?

The knock came again and Troylus rolled his eyes.

"I'm coming, keep your uniform on," he said, opening the door and leaning on the jam only to find himself inches from Zellendine, her fist raised in the air to knock again.

He froze. He should have stepped back, he should have shut the door, but any ability to move was stuck deep inside him, buried beneath the need that rose to the surface with a force like a collision of stars to take hold of the hand in front of him and ask her if she meant it. If she meant that he was as wrong as the anomaly.

"Zellendine." His voice was hoarse, her name came out of him sounding like a cry of pain.

"You are hard to find." She lowered her hand and flexed it out before she wrapped it around the holo she clutched to her chest.

"Didn't know you were looking." Troylus dropped his arm to his side and stared, unable to figure out what he was supposed to do.

She fidgeted and looked around, turning to see down both directions of the hallway before she shoved into the room past him and shut the door behind her.

"What in the universe do you think you're doing?" Troylus stepped back and grabbed the doorknob, about to fling it open again, but she put a hand on his arm, sending a jolt through him and he stopped.

"I know it isn't protocol, but no one needs to know, and I

need to talk to you. I have something to show you," she said, her eyes wide and her voice low. There was a quaver to it and the hand she held on his arm was trembling slightly.

"Are you okay?" He couldn't help it. He didn't want to give a shit and just send her on her way, but she seemed freaked out. He couldn't ignore that.

"No." She slumped, like she was holding herself straight up by will alone and his question had undone her.

"What happened?" He stepped forward, taking her hand off his arm to thread his fingers through hers and shrinking the distance between them. He didn't ask what was wrong, so much was wrong it would have been a ridiculous question, but something new must have happened, and with the way things had been going, a lump formed in his throat thinking about what that could be.

Zellendine squeezed her eyes shut and leaned her head against his chest, her hand tight on his as she dragged in a deep breath and let it out again.

He couldn't breathe, his chest was tight, and his heart was hammering, the blood rushing through his veins so he heard it in his head. Keeping his free arm at his side instead of wrapping it around her back and holding her close was a physical ache.

"You can tell me." His voice was a rough whisper and he couldn't take it anymore, he pulled her to him as she dragged in ragged breaths and clung to the front of his uniform. With his eyes tightly shut, he tried to let go of doubt and relish in the fact that she had come to him. "Whatever it is, Zellendine, I'm here."

"Troylus," she said, looking up at him, tears shining in her dark eyes.

He took his hand from hers and cupped her cheek, wiping away a tear with his thumb.

"Please don't cry." Something inside him cracked at seeing

her so despondent, especially when he had no idea what the cause was.

"Is there anything I can do? Can you tell me what's going on?" he asked, leading her to his bunk, protocol be damned, so she could sit down on the edge with him, still wrapped in his arms.

She sniffed and shook her head, her eyebrows high while her mouth opened and closed without any words and the tears came faster.

"Is it that bad?" he asked, the lump making his voice sound like it was struggling to come out.

"Yes. Troylus, it's impossible, but it's worse than..." She looked around and gestured at the empty air in front of her. "Anything. It's worse than anything I could have imagined."

"Zellendine, you're starting to really scare me," he said, although he didn't think she knew that he was scared for her more than he was scared about her news. He was concerned about her news, sure, but whatever it was, his primary concern was that it was hurting her.

"I..." She choked and coughed, curling into his chest and taking deliberate breaths before she tried again, holding the holo out toward him.

"I found something, and I think you need to see it and tell me I'm wrong, tell me it doesn't mean what I think it means."

43

ZELLENDINE

"Please?" she asked, shoving the holo toward him.

He unwrapped his arm from around her back and the lack of his support made her cold, goosebumps broke out across her skin, and her muscles ached as if she was sick. Which, in a way she was.

Troylus tapped the holo to life and squinted his shining silver eyes at the information she had found. He tapped back and forth and then kept going through the information at an ever increasing clip.

"Does this say what I think it does?" His voice was barely audible, but it was loud enough to confirm to her that she wasn't misreading it. She had not imagined the horror, it was real. He saw it too. He turned his silver eyes to her, pulling the holo away from his face like it was contagious.

"Yes." She didn't know what else to say. That one word was bad enough.

Before she could reach out and catch it, the holo dropped to the floor. Troylus's hands remained open in his lap as he stared down at it and tears welled in his eyes.

"I'm sorry, I didn't know what to do. I'm sorry I showed you. It's not fair... None..." Zellendine couldn't talk, she had no words. But Troylus turned to her, his face as horrified and drowned in sadness as she felt.

The vision of him blurred as her tears became too much.

He scooped her up and they clung to each other while they cried.

"How? How did they keep this from us? How did we not know?" Troylus said into her hair, his arms almost vibrating and his voice hardening as he spoke.

"I don't know." She shook her head against his chest, not letting go for even a second. "All I can think is that it doesn't happen on the same shift often enough to make people suspicious. And that no one wants to think about how sad it is for too long so they don't bother to look into it beyond doing maintenance on the wombs and assuming that it will never happen again."

"Keep moving forward fucking bullshit." Troylus's voice was a growl, but his hands on her back remained gentle and his hold on her kept her together.

"Yes." She did it again, ran out of words beyond just agreeing with him.

"We have to tell people," Troylus said and Zellendine went still and stiff in his arms.

He pulled back from her enough to look her in the eyes, his face awash in tears and his jaw set, his eyes hard.

"People on this ship need to know, Zellendine. I know you agree with that," he said, pausing and waiting until after she nodded her head to keep talking. "So we need to tell everyone what you found."

"No, Troylus, I broke the law to see it. How can I explain that away? Would people even believe me? I would be a criminal to them, they would probably think I made it all up to get out of trouble. No one would want to believe this. How would I begin to convince them?" she asked, shaking her head and turning to look down at the holo and the black hole it felt like it had become.

Troylus squeezed his eyes shut and grimaced. Taking a hand from her back to rub roughly against his face, he growled under his breath and swiped at the tears on his face.

"But how do we just sit on this? I mean, it's ten, fifteen percent?" he asked, staring into her eyes, his face wavering between horror, despair, and rage.

"We can't tell anyone," she started, and he opened his mouth like he was going to argue so she plowed ahead. "Listen, we are already putting the warning about the wombs and the new instructions that everyone has to be warned and for it to keep moving. I'm also going to add the warnings to all the first files that the medics use when they come on shift to see any specific notices that they would need. It's the only thing I can think to do without getting caught. I promise, I have thought about it."

He stared into her eyes, searching them, pouring the silver shine of them into her mind it seemed to hunt through her intentions.

She welcomed his inspection. She wasn't hiding anything from him. He was the one person on board the Wheel she was honest with.

Finally, Troylus dropped his eyes to the floor and tucked her into his side again, taking a deep shuddering breath as he did.

"It's worse than being wrong about assignments. I can't believe I was so worried about the fucked up assignments. Killing 10-15% of the babies as they're born is still worse." Troylus rubbed his hand over her back and the fire had gone out of his voice, replaced by a desperate sadness.

"What I still don't understand is, why? I thought I found a pattern when five in a row had a parent with diabetes, but it was just a statistical fluke." Zellendine turned her face into the warmth of his uniform and tried to slow the tears. It would have been easier if she had found an answer, but she was like a spaceship without a planet to head toward, facing vast darkness she didn't know if there was an end to.

"Five?" Troylus asked, leaning away from her to grab the holo again although he held it like it was dangerous.

"Yeah. But that pattern never happened again; although Anders has it too, it's been a while since one of the parents had it so I think it doesn't mean anything." She wrapped her arms around herself while he tapped at the holo in a slow, careful way. He still held it away from himself like he didn't really want to be touching it more than he had to. Or, maybe that was how she felt about the damn thing. She thought she might never look at the medic files the same way again.

"Are you looking for something specific?" she asked, her voice sounded far away to her own ears.

"How many of the parents did you look at?" he asked, tapping away, his back hunched and his face intent.

"Just the first thirty, the five occurred in the first ten, then I had the holo do a search through the rest for diabetes and it didn't pop up again but a couple times. Those same five couples eventually went on to have babies on their second try that survived." She held her eyes shut for a second, trying to will the tears back. When she opened them he was holding the holo out to her and she recoiled from it.

"Can you run a search for any genetic predispositions in the parents? Not just diabetes, but anything that might show up, but doesn't always?" he asked, putting a hand on her back, his face full of sadness.

"Why?" Zellendine did not understand what that would do, there were so many. "Practically everyone has something that they're genetically predisposed to."

"Humor me, please." He raised his eyebrows and tilted his head to her, still holding the holo out.

She bit her lip and took the holo, for the first time in her life, the familiar device felt foreign, heavier than it should have. But she tapped in the search parameters, although they seemed far too broad, so she added that the predispositions be highlighted, and whether the child shared that genetic coding or not.

The holo took only seconds to run through all the information, only seconds to return an answer, only seconds to change everything.

"No. Universe, please, no." Zellendine shook her head and started tapping at the holo in rapid fire, missing the correct word twice in her haste. She had to know. She had to know now.

44

TROYLUS

"WHAT? WHAT DID IT SAY?" HE LEANED OVER TO LOOK AT THE damn thing in her hands that he expected any second to tell him he was going to die in five minutes because the air around it even seemed sinister to him now, but he had to know what had turned her face as white as the metal floor in the birthing room.

She tapped one last time and then clutched the holo, her hands almost bending the thin round frame and her knuckles turning as white as her face.

The number zero with a percent sign formed in the blank space in the center of the circle and she dropped it, pulling her knees up to her chest on the bed and burying her face in them.

He didn't know what that number meant, what she had seen the first time she ran his search, but it didn't matter. Her reaction was too much for him to even ask about what the holo said at that second. So, he scooped her up in his arms, careful not to jostle her too much, as he moved her closer and ducked his head to lean his cheek against hers.

Zellendine's shoulders shook, her breathing was ragged and

there was a sound like a wail in the distance, barely perceptible, that followed her every exhale.

Troylus didn't know what the number meant, but her anguish, and knowing what he already did, that so many babies were being killed by the very machines they all relied on to survive just as they were about to live, made his own tears fall down his face.

"Come on, Zellendine. You can tell me. What is it? How bad?" he whispered near her ear.

She shook, a tremor running through her and she pulled back from him. He stared into her eyes as she unwrapped her arms from around her legs and dropped her knees. She put a hand on his cheek while she cried and her mouth worked. It seemed to him like she was struggling to get out the words.

"The Chapter did it, Troylus."

He swallowed and nodded, expecting that the Chapter computer had been what doomed the babies at the very moment of birth without warning that anything was wrong, but he didn't know how she was so sure. She took a deep, shaky breath. "The computer killed every baby that had a genetic predisposition. There isn't a single baby born with genetic mutations anymore other than green eyes because the Chapter filters it out in the samples, but this is next level and there is no way for the computer to know until after the fetus has started developing further, but that doesn't make sense out of why it waits until the baby is about to be born. It's just so cruel."

"Anders would never forgive himself if he knew that it was a connection to him that the fucking computer didn't like." Troylus shook his head and exhaled a long sigh, squeezing his eyes shut. "So, the Chapter's little tests on the samples just wasn't enough for them. They have to do this too. Damn, and if Anders and Yanna had waited until they could have their kids the old fashioned way on the planet, the computer wouldn't get a damn say."

"No, but a lot of people are worried they will have long term fertility issues like some people did when they landed on the last planet," Zellendine said and Troylus's eyebrows shot up.

"Oh, really? Isn't that some pretty damn far looking back?" he asked, one corner of his mouth twitching up as a smile played with him, although he didn't feel happy at all.

"It's for medical purposes of warning people, we have to go over everything with those that come in and discuss using the wombs. The thing is, this," she said, waving her hand toward the holo on the floor, "isn't part of the information we give them. It isn't part of the information we know to give them."

Troylus rubbed a hand over his face and Zellendine took a hold of his other one. Both of them had stopped crying, but the shock, the feeling of turning around and seeing a flag flying right for the ship, was clinging to him and it looked to him like it was doing the same to her.

"What do we do with this?" he asked, lost for any idea of what to do with the weight they were both carrying.

"Nothing," she said and dropped her head into her hand. "Nothing at all."

Part of him wanted to argue. Hell, part of him wanted to storm into the quarters of every single person in leadership and demand they answer whether they knew or not and put the word out to the rest of the Chapter ships... but he knew better than that.

"I get why we can't say anything. I do. But..." he trailed off and turned to stare at the wall, not really knowing what he was about to say, only knowing that none of it was right or fair, and he was highly unqualified to try and rectify the situation.

"But what?" she asked, her voice quiet and when he turned

back to her, she was looking at him as if she was going to fall asleep sitting up.

"You need to get some sleep," he said, rather than answering her question.

"I'm fine." She waved away his concerns, but it was accompanied by a yawn so it wasn't convincing at all.

"No, you're not. And even if you were, Rullon will be back from Indigo's soon." He got up from the edge of the bed and held a hand out to her. "Come on."

Her shoulders slumped and a tremulous smiled formed on her lips, but before she took his hand she reached down and picked up the holo.

Troylus pulled her to her feet and wrapped her in his arms for a hug again. She did need to go to her own quarters, and he wasn't sure he could take talking in circles about what, if anything, they should do with the terrible information they had about the group that was the foundation of their whole world, but none of that was why he was sending her away. He did it because he had to think, he had to process. And as long as Zellendine was around, all of his thoughts would be filtered through his concern for her.

Before he walked her to her quarters, though, he held her. His chin rested on her head while they clung to each other, and he waited until both of them were breathing steadily and he thought he could let her go for the night without worrying if something worse was going to happen.

4 5

ZELLENDINE

THE NEXT DAY, AFTER NOT SLEEPING MUCH THE NIGHT BEFORE, Zellendine went through the motions at the clinic. But every step, every time she called her own dad, Stephen for protocol, or entered something in a holo, she had to swallow and fight the roiling in her stomach so she didn't vomit.

She was still playing the perfect daughter of the Chapter, but it had never felt more like a betrayal of everyone and everything that really mattered to her.

Just before the meal break chime was going to come over the intercom, Troylus popped up in an exam room.

Zellendine glanced around before she went into the exam room and shut the door behind herself.

"What are you doing here?" she asked, crossing the room to wrap him in a hug and taking what felt like her first full breath of the day. For as long as he was around, she didn't have to pretend.

"I wanted to see how you were doing," he said, his voice low and calm like he was singing her a lullaby.

"Can you eat with me and take a break?" she asked, but she

didn't let go of him or even look at him, she kept her face buried in his neck.

"That's why I'm here, Zellendine. I mean, you can give me an exam, or check my eyes, or something, if that would make you feel better." He chuckled, low and soft, so she did too. It was a balm to her overwrought mind and a break for her entire body to be with him. Her muscles unclenched and she was finally able to take a deep breath. Until she remembered that the only reason he was comfort to her was because he knew, and knowing put him at risk.

She pulled away from him, but he hung on and she wilted.

"Zellendine, I just had an idea." His silver eyes shown, and a smile was even teasing the corners of his mouth.

"Okay," she said, her heart starting to pound.

"I've been running through this in my head every second and I think I may have a solution, a way to stop the Chapter eventually," he said, his smile growing larger with a sinister edge to it.

"How?" she asked, grabbing onto his uniform, the fabric bunched in her fists as her hope soared even while her brain tried to tell it not to.

"We can't do it until we get to the planet."

She started to pull away, her hope withering, because so many more people would be risking the grief Yanna and Anders were going through between that moment and the ship's arrival.

Troylus grabbed her hand as she backed up, stopping her retreat.

"I know that's disappointing, but you've put in the warning, and we can't risk leadership finding out what we know and shutting us down, even stopping us from going to the planet at all." He rushed through his words and his smile vanished, replaced with the fear she recognized from her own reflection.

"So, what do we do? We can't let this go on forever. They're engineering the people through a damn computer system." Her voice was colder and angrier than she expected it to be, but she realized she was mad. There wasn't just grief and she wasn't just lost. She was pissed off.

"When we're off this damn ship, we send a message to every single Chapter ship, embed it in an update from the medic crew about the health of everyone after terraforming and initial colonizing and in the update from the starwalkers about the building program." His eyes took on the gleam of brutal hope again and Zellendine bit her lip, trying not to get her hopes up too.

"Okay, but most of the reports go to leadership on all the other ships. They'll bury them." She closed her eyes until he squeezed her hand, his face not losing its savage glee.

"Not all the reports go direct to leadership. We put the message in those and in the other ones, so even if they try and filter them, it won't work. They won't know about the ones in the wide messages and they'll be confronted with questions from the people, regardless of whether they try and cover it up."

"But what do we do about these wombs? The ones on this ship? People will still use them, and eventually the ship will take off again and then everyone will be at the mercy of them again." She shook her head.

"We sabotage the computer system," he said, like what he was suggesting made sense and he couldn't believe she didn't think the same.

"No one can sabotage the system, I don't even know how to access it."

"Just because no one has tried, doesn't mean it's impossible. And if we can't stop the computer, then we destroy it so it can't be used again for the wombs or the assignments." He smiled and looked genuinely happy.

"Why are you smiling? If we destroy the computers, then no one who needs the wombs can use them. That isn't a solution."

She pulled her hand out of his and crossed her arms over her chest, chewing on her lip.

"Because, that's just it; the wombs, the machines, the comms, everything will still work, but it won't have the programming. The robotics department can make it do what it needs to without any interference at all. Even the matching of the samples, there's a database, it could be done by hand. More work for you, but none for the Chapter." He stood up and crossed to her, taking her hands from where they had dropped to her sides.

Her mouth opened to argue, her brain ran through the possibilities at break neck speed, sure that there was something they were missing, some way in which they relied on the Chapter and their computers. But she couldn't think of any.

"Everyone relies on them because we're used to it. We would have to come up with a whole new way to do everything, even assignments," she said, her voice low and awed by the possibilities and challenges.

"But we don't need to rely on them. We can do this. You and I can make this real. We could even get Briar to help us imbed a message in the terraforming department's reports," he said, smiling a bright conspiratorial smile that made her think of the time they all skipped class to hide in the orchard and play all day.

For her, though, even thinking of Briar, the boy she grew up with or the man she knew, dropped her heart into her stomach. She dropped her eyes to the floor and grimaced.

"He can't know," she said. Her words shot a sharp stab through her.

Troylus dropped her hands and stepped back from her, his brow furrowed and his smile gone. "Why not?"

Zellendine raised her eyes to his, locking her gaze with his silver one that no longer seemed as strange as it used to.

"Are you sure he wouldn't turn us in? Even when we get to the planet, are you willing to risk retribution? I'm not sure I am." Her voice gave out and the part of her that had shoved Briar to the back of her mind, the part of her that had led to her avoiding him, was screaming.

"But… he's going to be your partner," Troylus said, shaking his head.

Maybe not, she wanted to say. But the words caught in her throat.

46

TROYLUS

"I... should get back to work," Zellendine said and turned away from him. She walked out of the exam room leaving the door open behind her and him standing in the middle of the room still unsure where in the universe he had been transported to.

"There's no way," he muttered to the empty room and wandered out, paying no attention to anyone or anything other than that he didn't see Zellendine.

Back at the starwalker office he slumped in a chair, not hearing half of the conversations going on around him.

What had she meant? Why wouldn't they be able to trust Briar? How could she be partners with someone she couldn't trust? Somehow, he had assumed she would tell Briar when they got to the planet. That was the only thing that made any sense.

"Hey, how is all that coming with the sleepers?" Rullon asked, his voice managing to penetrate the haze in Troylus's mind.

"Zellendine is running her tests and I think she'll figure it out soon, but I'm not really in the loop." About anything.

"You have to know more than that, you're with her all the time," Maurice said, before he put a hand to his ear and started talking to Parmita out on her starwalk.

Rullon looked over at him with a frown on his face.

Troylus focused back on his holo and the work he was pretending to do. In no universe did he want to talk to Rullon about Zellendine in front of Maurice with the whole rest of the crew listening through the comm.

Besides, he wasn't even sure what there was to say. His feelings for her got more complicated by the day and in the meantime she was in love enough with Briar to think it didn't matter that she didn't trust him and that she thought he wasn't in love enough with her not to turn her in.

Low blow, that.

So, he tried to fake like he was fine. He tried to fake like he had not found out the worst about the Chapters. He tried to fake that it wasn't unnerving to be out in space, more than one hundred years from landing, and that he wasn't sure anymore if they were going to be able to wake the sleepers or help the wombs, or stop the Chapters.

Very little seemed sure to him at that moment and he let all the things that were spinning without an orbit or clear trajectory twist his mind down wormholes that just led in loops.

"Maurice," Rullon said, his voice hoarse and low, his eyes riveted on the flag map.

Next to him, Maurice turned his way and his face fell.

"A flag?" he asked.

"Tell the crew nothing is wrong and turn off your comm," Rullon said, the color draining from his face.

Maurice followed the order and leaned over to stare at the flag map in front of Rullon. His hand dropped limply to his side.

"What?" Troylus asked, putting his holo down even though the two men blocked his view of the map.

They didn't answer, just stared mute and still at the map in front of them.

"Seriously," Troylus said, "what the hell is going on?"

Rullon turned toward him, his mouth open and working around silent words while his eyes were huge.

Clearly, they weren't going to tell him, so he stood up and leaned over them both.

At first, he wasn't sure what the issue was. The map was clear of flags.

But… wait. He was wrong. There was a flag. A giant flag in a single, undulating band along the bottom of the map, following the ship at a steady pace. The anomaly was back.

He dropped the holo in his hands and sprinted from the room. As far as he knew there was exactly one person onboard the Wheel the anomaly didn't like. He had to find her. He had to keep her away from the windows.

47

─────────

ZELLENDINE

She shoved Troylus to the back of her mind, again, and checked the holo for her next patient waiting for her.

Yanna.

For some reason, it never occurred to her that Yanna would want to see her, especially after she and Anders went to her father. It made more sense for them to see someone else, but she couldn't turn Yanna away and Stephen and the other medics were in with other patients. No matter how unprepared she was to help Yanna, she was going to have to figure it out.

"Okay. Professional. I am a professional and I am here for her," Zellendine said, nodding her head and standing up straight before she opened the door to the exam room and tried for a smile she hoped looked encouraging.

"Hi, Yanna," she said, perching on the chair in the room. "How are you?"

Yanna turned her cold stare from her feet to Zellendine. Her skin was splotchy with red patches like hives and her nails were bitten down to the quick, her hair was pulled back in a severe bun, so plastered down flat it looked like it hurt her scalp.

"I'm surprised you even showed; aren't you busy with waking your partner's brother?" Yanna asked, her voice hard.

Zellendine swallowed and licked her lips, buying time while she formulated her answer.

"We have been trying to wake those sleeping. Unfortunately, we haven't found the answer yet. Although, I hope to have a way to do that soon after I'm finished with the tests I'm doing." Yanna narrowed her eyes and Zellendine tightened her grip on the holo in her lap. "Now, what brings you in today?"

"Maybe just to see if I was right." Yanna leaned forward like she was about to leap from her chair and wrap the hands she was wringing together around Zellendine's neck.

Stop it. She wasn't going to attack, Zellendine told herself.

"Right about what?" Zellendine's voice squeaked and Yanna's mouth turned up into a vicious smile.

"That you weren't doing a damn thing to find out what happened to my baby. You have nothing to do with the sleepers but that's not stopping you from devoting all your time to them while you do nothing for what you are responsible for, my dead baby." Yanna's voice cracked on dead and every word out of her mouth was another sharp stab into Zellendine's heart.

"I promise I have been looking. I swear…" Zellendine's voice gave out and a tear managed to get through her lashes and drip down her cheek. No wonder Yanna was so angry with her, she was looking to blame someone because she was trying so hard not to blame herself. She swiped at her eye and rushed to assure Yanna. "But it wasn't my fault or yours or anyone's. The computers did it like they did before."

Yanna reared back, her mouth falling open and her eyes going wide while Zellendine froze and screamed inside her mind.

What just happened? Did she just let that slip? What was she doing?

"How do you know it was the computer?" Yanna whispered. The hate in her voice made the hair on Zellendine's arms stand on end.

"I..." Lies caught in Zellendine's throat and she couldn't go on. She couldn't even refute what she had let slip. Part of her was screaming to cover her ass, the rest of her was wailing in grief and didn't want to make it worse for the woman sitting in front of her.

"You said, before. I don't know of any others except for one years ago. How do you know?" Yanna's voice was still a whisper but it was so loud inside Zellendine's head she couldn't move.

"Zellendine," Troylus said, barreling into the room and collapsing at her side, running his hands over her shoulders and looking her up and down like he was checking to see if she was all there.

"What are you doing here?" she managed to ask around the lump in her throat.

"The anomaly is back," he said, letting that be all the warning he would give, his eyes darting over to take in Yanna.

She sat up and looked out the door at the one across from the room she was in. It was closed, but the exam room on the other side had a window.

Her heart raced in her chest and she jumped up from the chair to stand behind the open door to the exam room, letting it shield her from the hallway, and burying her face in her hands.

"But it's defended the ship too, right?" she asked, her voice tremulous and her tears threatening again.

"I don't trust it around you. And last time it wasn't stalking the ship the way it is now. I just want you to stay away from the windows," Troylus said, pulling her into a hug so she could rest her head on his chest.

"Wait, where's Yanna?" she asked, looking past him, but Yanna was gone.

"Oh, no. Troylus, I may have screwed up." She looked up into his silver eyes and wrapped her arms around him, holding him tight. He had come to her, to warn her. Not only did she need to protect him, being held in the safety of his arms was beginning to be the only place on board she felt safe.

"How did you screw up? I'm sure it's not as bad as you think," he said, giving her a small smile.

"No, it's probably worse. I just want you to do me a favor, if leadership comes for me, let me go. If you're in trouble too, I think I might fall apart."

Troylus stiffened and looked around like someone was going to come and collect her at that second, but his hands on her back were gentle, and when he reached up to tuck her head under his chin he did it slowly and with care.

"It's not going to happen. I won't let it," he said.

She was sure he meant it, but there wasn't a damn thing he could do to stop it, and every second she spent further from Yanna's rage filled face felt like it was borrowed time.

48

TROYLUS

HE DIDN'T WANT TO LET HER GO. HE DIDN'T WANT TO GO BACK to the starwalker office. He sure as hell didn't want to just wait around for leadership to come and get her, but he was walking down the hallway back to work, alone.

Why the hell did he listen to her, he wanted to know. His hands were in fists at his sides and his footfalls were heavy. It was everything he could do not to go back to her, but she was right that she needed to work and he needed to keep an eye on the anomaly and get some of the shields closed up.

"Is everything okay?" Rullon asked as he slumped into a chair in the office.

"Everybody's on break?" he asked instead of answering because no, everything was not okay, but he couldn't explain that to his dad.

"Yeah, they're bringing me food. Did you eat?" Rullon kept his eyes on the map in front of him, not bothering to look at him, which made sense to Troylus. It's not like he was telling his dad the truth.

"Hey, I need to do a walk, can you be on comms for me?" he

asked, shoving up from the chair and not waiting for his dad to say anything. He would do it, even if he didn't want to.

Putting on his suit, he took a minute to hope that Yanna wouldn't say anything and that his plan to derail the Chapters would work. It had to work. And he couldn't think about what would happen if Yanna did say something. He couldn't. It was impossible.

So, instead, the only thing he could do was to protect Zellendine the way he knew how to. The only thing he could do was to close some shields and be with her in the hours they weren't working.

Maybe he didn't offer much in the way of help for the sleepers, but he was going to be with her in the cryo bay every damn time she was there until he was sure that leadership wasn't coming for her.

The airlock opened and Troylus stepped into space. He stared out behind the ship and focused toward the sun.

Sure enough, the anomaly wavering showed in the same way it had before.

"What the hell *are* you?" he asked the void of space.

"Troylus?" Rullon's voice came through the comms and he shook his head at himself.

"Never mind, I was just talking to the thing. Maybe I should have Zellendine do a mental check on me." He laughed at himself without humor and grabbed a handhold, pulling himself over to the clinic windows first.

He shut them all, there was no way that damn thing would get her in the place she couldn't avoid. He wasn't going to let leadership attack her and some damn space nuisance wasn't going to get to her either. Not if he could help it.

Using the handholds, he tracked what would be her path from the clinic to her quarters, closing any window that looked on the hallway.

It took him a few minutes of peering in windows to orient himself to the layout of the inside of the ship to his place clinging to the outside.

Once he figured it out, he tracked the way from the cryo bay with the sleepers still resting, blissfully unaware that so much was going on around them.

He took a second to stare in at them, to wonder what they were dreaming about.

"Rullon?" he asked, looking from Upton to the wizened face of Grandma Elisa.

"Yeah?"

"How old is Grandma Elisa?" he asked, noticing that they all looked serene which made him hope they were all having pleasant dreams.

"Grandma Elisa and Grandpa Kason are two of the oldest people on board, but I don't think I know what their exact age is."

"No?" Troylus shut the shield and pulled himself along to the next window on the way to the clinic from the cryo bay.

"Well, I think she's older than Grandpa Kason by a few days, but that's all the details I know." Rullon's voice rattled around in his head even more than it usually did on a walk.

"The youngest and the oldest," he muttered to himself.

"Youngest and oldest of what?" Rullon asked and Troylus shook his head.

He had to stop saying his thoughts out loud when he was on a damn comm, he thought as he shut the shield on the cryo bay and moved along the windows of the corridor connecting the bay to the clinic.

"One more," he said, pulling himself along by the handholds, not bothering to rush as the weight of his hours of concern for Zellendine gave way to exhaustion.

He grabbed the shield on the last window and pulled it closed.

But… What was that?

Troylus flung the shield back open so hard it slammed and bounced back so he had to catch it.

Just beyond the window, Zellendine was being led down the hall by two members of leadership, her hands twisting together in front of her and her lip between her teeth while his heart snapped its tether and plummeted to his feet.

He smacked his hand against the window, knowing the likelihood that any of them would hear him through the massive frame of the ship and his gloves muting the sound of the impact was slim to none.

But, damn it, she had to look at him. She just had to. He needed to know if this was everything they had worried about. He needed to know how much destruction he was going to have to commit in order to fight this.

His breaths were ragged and the blood rushing through him pounded in his ears.

"Come on, Zellendine, look at me. Please," he yelled at the window.

Zellendine's step faltered and she looked up even as the people flanking her showed no sign they had heard a thing.

She didn't stop walking, but she slowed, and he thought she was trying to give him an extra few seconds trying to puzzle out of her guarded expression what exactly had happened. He didn't need the extra time.

Eyes huge, lip trembling where it was trapped between her teeth, entire body straight and taught like she was going to snap, and a tiny line between her brows all told him that fear was actually walking her down the hallway, the people on either side of her were just stand ins.

"Damn it. Shit. Okay, Zellendine." He put his hand to the

window and nodded, hoping she could see him through his helmet. "I'll figure a way to get you out. I won't let this happen."

Her teeth didn't let go of her bottom lip, but the corners of her mouth turned up a fraction and she shook her head an even tinier amount.

"I don't care what you say, you can't stop me." Both his hands pressed against the window and he stayed until she turned and went down a corridor he couldn't see into.

A tiny voice in his head reminded him of all the shields he had already shut and that they could be open since she wasn't going to be passing by them anytime soon.

"Screw it. They can stay shut," he said, pulling himself along the handholds back toward the airlock.

49

ZELLENDINE

Seeing Troylus through the window was both what she wanted, and the last thing she needed. Thank the universe she had the chance to give him even the smallest reminder to stay clear of the whole mess. He had to save himself to save everyone else. But his hands pressed against the window like he wanted to reach through it and take her away from the situation she was in... it was all she could do to keep her back straight and her feet moving.

The door to the gathering room loomed before her, more ominous than the last time she had walked through it. Last time she had looked at the door and the leadership team as people she wanted to impress, now she looked at them as people who didn't care if what she was doing was the right thing if it went against their orders.

Well, screw them, she thought as she crossed the threshold into the meeting room, allowing herself only a second to be surprised that Grandpa Kason and Alara were the only people in the room.

"Hello, Zellendine," Alara said, her tone was kind and her

smile almost seemed real, but Zellendine told herself not to believe it.

Of all the things the computer programs systematic killing said about the leadership, the Chapter system, and her entire world, the biggest lesson for her was that it was all a lie and she couldn't trust anyone in power.

"Hello, I think I am making progress on helping the sleepers if that's what this is about," she said even though she felt further from the truth every day. Her scans of herself, and Briar had yielded no help. It would do her no good to admit anything and her only play was to pretend she didn't know why they had yanked her out of the clinic in the middle of an appointment.

"A progress report isn't necessary at this point, Stephen will be taking over that avenue of inquiry," Grandpa Kason said, leaning toward her and narrowing his eyes.

She swallowed and tried to paint her face in naivete with a small smile and her eyes only vaguely interested.

"Oh, well, that probably makes sense. He has a lot more experience than I do, but I'm glad I was able to help. I just want everyone to be okay." She left off that in order for that to happen she was plotting against the people standing in front of her. Admitting that for sure wouldn't help. Her small smile grew more real as she tried to bury her inappropriate urges to tell them the truth.

"Do you?" Grandpa Kason asked, his eyes only further narrowing.

"Zellendine," Alara said, shooting Grandpa Kason a look and pulling herself up to her full height which made her more regal and terrifying, "I'm afraid this change is because we have received a serious charge against you."

"Against me?" her voice squeaked as she said it, but she hoped it made her look more innocent instead of the opposite.

"Yes. It's serious enough that we need to separate you while we learn what kind of influence you have exerted over your ship mates." Alara's voice wasn't hard, but what she said made the hair rise on Zellendine's arms.

Influence, as if they were going to hunt down whoever she had contact with and see if they were swayed too much. Troylus. If they went to him he was going to do something rash and she needed him to be okay, to keep going.

The small of her back started to sweat with the effort to leave her face blank while her mind screamed to run, protect Troylus, warn him, punch someone, anything. Anything other than the only thing she could do, which was nothing.

5 0

TROYLUS

THE AIRLOCK HAD NEVER TAKEN SO DAMN LONG. HE CURLED HIS hands into fists to stop himself from pulling apart his suit before it was safe.

Finally, the light changed, and the door opened. He was pulling off his helmet as he stepped through the door.

Rullon was in front of him, his mouth in a thin line and his hands on his hips.

"Maurice and the others are in the office, you are coming with me," Rullon said.

"No, I can't. I have to - " Troylus started, but stopped when Rullon raised a hand.

"I know what you think you have to do, go after her." Rullon raised an eyebrow and Troylus froze for a second.

Shit, what did he say when he was out there? Had he turned off his comm? By the look on Rullon's face, Troylus guessed he was distracted enough not to turn off his comm and that his dad heard everything.

"But," Rullon continued, "I'm telling you what you're going to do is come with me first."

"Please, you don't understand," Troylus said, willing to get on his hands and knees to have Rullon let him go. He had to get to her.

"I understand enough to know you're not thinking and you're coming with me before you do something stupid. Now, put your stuff away." Rullon crossed his arms over his chest and Troylus wanted to scream. Fine. He would go with his dad, but the second he got done he was going after Zellendine.

Troylus pulled off the rest of his suit and followed after Rullon in silence.

Down the corridors they went, his hands were still in fists and he couldn't help but look down every offshoot they passed and through every open door. He didn't know where leadership had taken her. He couldn't remember a time that someone had been banned from colonizing. He couldn't even remember a time that someone had been sanctioned by the leadership, everyone just knew what would happen if they ever were. Somewhere along the way he must have heard the stories of other people being punished, but he couldn't remember where they came from. It didn't matter though, because he believed them to be truth. And nothing about the look on Zellendine's face told him he was wrong.

Blonde hair made him stop in his tracks. But it wasn't her.

Troylus took a breath that hitched and shot pain through his heart, leaving him fighting to hold the tears locked away while he picked up his pace to catch up with Rullon. Whatever his dad wanted, he had to make it fast.

Rullon led him to their quarters where he shut the door behind Troylus and rounded on him, the light in his eyes was as close to untethered as Troylus had ever seen him and his jowls shook as he worked up to saying what he needed to.

After his mother died, it took Rullon a long time to work up the words to talk about the loss with Troylus and Indigo. He looked like he was going through the same thing to Troylus and he knew the only way to help him get the words out was to wait. Which sucked.

No matter how hard he tried to be patient, his eyes kept roaming to the door, wondering where Zellendine was on the other side and what he was going to do to help her.

"What did you do?" Rullon asked, his face clear of all the strain and instead painted in grim determination.

"I don't know what you mean." By the look on Rullon's face, his lips pursed out and his eyes narrowed, Troylus didn't think that was going to work, but he had to try.

"Bullshit. You and Zellendine did something. One minute you're out there talking about you not letting something happen and getting her out and the next damn minute Maurice and Parmita come in to tell me they heard Zellendine is going on trial in a couple days." Rullon walked across the room to sit at the table and rubbed a hand over his face while the floor fell away under Troylus and he felt like he was left in the middle of space so far from the ship he forgot what it looked like.

"On trial?" he asked, dropping to the ground to sit where he was in the middle of the room, his legs not able to even bring him to a chair. Rullon nodded. It was worse than he even thought it was.

"Listen," Rullon said, "they're going to want to talk to you, for you to testify."

Something inside Troylus snapped and he cried out as he buried his face in his hands and grabbed at his hair.

"They've got her locked up because I helped her. Damn it." Troylus looked up at his dad who sat as stone faced as before and knew he had to tell him. If it meant he would condemn Troylus, then fine, but he didn't think Rullon would turn him in. "We were trying to find a way to help the sleepers and see if the problem with the womb was connected somehow. So, we looked back."

Rullon only raised an eyebrow at that but otherwise stayed still and listening.

"I showed her how we look back on the map in the office and she followed along on her holo in the medic files. We found out the Chapter computers are killing the babies as they're born that they deem possibly may develop health challenges."

Rullon sucked in a breath and covered his mouth with a fist, only partially hiding his grimace.

"Exactly." Troylus nodded. "We came up with a plan to do something about it once we all get down to the planet because we didn't want to get stuck on the ship, and now…" He trailed off and then couldn't help but laugh earning him a dirty look from his dad. "Sorry, it's just that I don't even know if she found something to help wake up the sleepers or not. She only told me about the wombs. I'm pretty sure she would have told me if she had found good news so it was probably all for naught."

"Stop it," Rullon said, pointing a finger at Troylus. "You two uncovered something that does need to be fixed and figured out a way to do it. It wasn't for nothing. Now, you need to figure out a way to help her the same way you figured out how to stop the computers. In a way that works and manages to get her out of trouble without you getting into trouble."

"Dad," Troylus said, although he rarely called him that, "I don't care about me right now. I just want her to be okay and to get to the planet."

"Yeah, I know you love her, but I think you would both be happier if you could be on the planet together, don't you?" Rullon asked, leaving Troylus tripping in his mind over the word love.

"As a friend. I love her as a friend."

"Okay, sure, kid. Well, as a friend you feel extra responsible for and protective of, or as something else, either way, I'm not wrong. And you're not stupid. So figure it out."

ZELLENDINE

In her worst nightmares, this was how it happened. The very reason she was afraid to look back, the exact reason she didn't want to tell anyone, to tell Briar, or expose Troylus to what she was doing. This was why. This moment.

Zellendine waited in the tiny closet turned holding room while the leadership crew prepared for her hearing. The light was dim, there was barely room for her and the chair she was sitting on to fit inside the not quiet space. Maybe it was supposed to be part of the punishment, to be put in a small box while you awaited the judgement of others, but she found herself leaning against the wall and fighting to stay awake.

No matter what they decided her punishment would be, it didn't matter, she had done the right thing. And though she still wasn't sure if she was going to claim that, or lie, she was sure that her actions up to the moment she was led to the closet were the right ones.

The sound of many voices filtered through the closed door and she sat up straighter in the chair expecting it to open. But it didn't. Instead, she rubbed her hands over her face to wake up and strained to hear what was being said on the other side.

Whatever the leadership decided, they would have to do it quick. They were running out of time to wake the sleepers before they were to go into stasis and after everything she risked to get them awake, she didn't trust anyone else to do the same.

She leaned forward and put her chin in her hand, trying to get more comfortable in the cramped space, but the door flew open before she could settle in and she sat up, blinking at the person silhouetted by the brighter light of the meeting room beyond.

"We're ready for you now," Alara said, her voice kind, betraying nothing of the severity of what was about to happen.

Zellendine stood up, maneuvering around the chair to squeeze out of the door past Alara.

The meeting room was full. Both leadership crews, the one from her shift, as well as the one from Briar's shift, were crammed onto the dais while members of both shifts not in leadership were seated on the floor of the main space.

Alara walked toward the amassed leadership, motioning for Zellendine to follow.

Even if she thought she was prepared for this while she sat alone, her steps felt like she was in heightened gravity on the way to the dais. Each one dragged her down and she fought for every inch forward, consciously making her legs move.

In the crowd, she spotted Yanna and Anders. Yanna bared her teeth in a snarl, her eyes held more power than their longest range telescopes into space. Anders had lost weight and looked even more fragile than the last time she saw him. He didn't make eye contact with her. Instead, he stared at the floor, seeming to barely register what was going on around him.

Stephen sat nearby, his hands clasped together in front of

him, looking for all the universe like he was waiting for a meal and not for the leadership to pass judgement on his daughter.

But Zellendine could see that his hands gripped each other so tightly his knuckles were white, and his fingers were red in places.

She swallowed, forcing her feet to carry her forward, forcing them to move in a steady pace to not show to the rest of the assembled people that she was worried. As much as she didn't know about the case against her, what they had, how it started, she figured the only way to the other side of the charges, whatever that looked like, was to pretend she was innocent and not worried about the outcome.

Her eyes though, while she kept her pace steady, her hands unclenched at her sides, she couldn't stop scanning the crowd, looking for Briar and Troylus, looking for Journo and Rullon. She couldn't stop hoping to see another friendly face besides her father.

Until she was seated on the dais, back straight and hands on her lap, she kept looking. Until it was clear they weren't there. Something inside her crumbled and it was no longer a fight to keep her hands from shaking, they sat lifeless. The part of her hoping for a positive outcome, a way for her to get leniency, or even cleared, was wiped away.

At least her surety of being found guilty made her worry disappear. She thought maybe that was a kindness from the universe, but maybe it was just another unexpected blow she would feel later. She tried to believe in the kindness.

"Zellendine," Alara said, her voice quiet and soft so that the whole of the room leaned forward and hushed their mumbled conversations to hear her speak, "You are called before leadership to answer the charges against you. Were you told of those charges?"

Part of her wanted to laugh, of course she was told the base charge, but details? Not hardly.

"Yes," she said, keeping her voice neutral and not bothering to complain about how little she did know.

"And what were the charges?" Alara asked, not looking at her, but facing the crowd.

Really? Zellendine thought. They wanted her to be the one to say it?

She took a deep breath before answering, aware of every set of eyes fastened on her.

"I am accused of looking back." The words landed like a comet flag they couldn't avoid. People sucked in their breaths, some recoiled like she slapped them. Yanna nodded, her smile growing more bitter, Anders hung his head, reacting for the first time like he heard her. Stephen, her own father, simply blinked, long and slow.

"In order to understand the complaint, we're first going to hear from Briar," Alara said. "You may ask him questions once we are done asking ours."

The door to the meeting room opened and Briar walked in, his face blank, Journo walking beside him. He made his way to the dais and stood near Alara, not facing Zellendine.

She didn't know what he was going to say, she didn't know what it meant that he wouldn't look at her, or that Journo was standing to the side, staring at his son.

"Briar," Grandpa Kason said, pulling himself up to stand next to Alara. "First let me say, I'm sorry that Upton still isn't awake, I know I hope every day that he, Elisa, and the other sleepers wake up and join us."

Many in the crowd nodded, some looked like they were about to cry. Zellendine wasn't sure if it was a good thing or not. Yes, she was the person most visible in the effort to wake up the sleepers, but she hadn't succeeded yet. Some of them might blame her for that.

"Thank you," Briar said, his eyes downcast.

"Our first question is, unfortunately, going to bring you back to that first shocking day out of stasis. What we need to know is about Zellendine's actions then, what did she tell you about how she was going to search for an answer to help your brother?" Grandpa Kason asked.

"She was nervous, she's not yet out of apprenticeship. Not really. She was worried, I was worried, Troylus was worried, all of us, just worried what it meant and at a loss to how we were going to save my brother and the others still sleeping. Plus, we were all worried about what would happen the next time we were supposed to go into stasis."

"Next time?" Alara asked, her eyebrow arched.

"Well, of course, looking forward meant we only had a month to find answers so it would be safe for Zellendine's shift to get into the tanks. What if it was the tanks themselves? We all want to see the new planet," Briar said, a tremulous smile played on his lips. Like he was almost wistful thinking about it, although Zellendine couldn't think of a less appropriate time to be wistful.

"A serious concern. It might have been understandable then that Zellendine, in a panic to solve the problem, thought about looking back?" Alara asked, her voice tinged in understanding.

"Zellendine would never think to do that. She follows all the laws of the Chapter and always works to be a good citizen of the Wheel." Briar shook his head, any possible smile falling from his face, while the roiling inside Zellendine's stomach grew worse. She wasn't what Briar was making her out to be, not anymore. Did he really think those things about her?

"Briar, you and Zellendine have been talking about becoming partners, is that right?" Grandpa Kason asked.

"Yes. I hope that once we reach the planet, we will be part-ners." His admission wasn't entirely unexpected, and at the beginning of the shift Zellendine would have said the same, but after what he said… she wasn't sure if she was even the girl he was talking about. She tried her damnedest not to think that Troylus was part of the reason she was suddenly questioning having Briar as a partner.

"Hmmm, well, that poses a problem for us regarding your veracity," Alara said, raising a hand in the stop motion when Briar opened his mouth to speak. He shut it again and Alara continued. "I understand that you think you're telling the truth, but you can't be impartial when it comes to the woman you want to have as a partner. You may be giving her the benefit of the doubt when she doesn't deserve it."

"I think it's time to call in Troylus," Grandpa Kason said before Briar could open his mouth again.

Zellendine's whole body felt the increased gravity again. From the top of her head to her toes, the weight on her increased. Troylus, who was livid with her at random since the shift began, and who absolutely did know that she broke the law was going to give witness, and if it had been the beginning of the shift she would have said he was bound to throw her into space without a suit. Troylus, who she wondered if he was going to do something idiotic and brave and put the blame on himself so she could get out of consequences, and who at the best of times wasn't a model citizen of the Wheel, was going to answer pointed questions from people in leadership he didn't trust. Troylus, who held her and cried with her and wanted to hurt the people responsible for both of their tears. Troylus, who could remake reality with his blue magic.

She had no idea what he was going to say.

5 2

TROYLUS

ONE OF THE PANELS IN THE HALLWAY OUTSIDE THE MEETING room was pulling away from the one next to it, their seam failing. Troylus could see through the gap to a bundle of wires inside the wall. Something in the wires called to him, like he could hear them.

It must have been his imagination trying to distract him from what was happening on the other side of the door to Zellendine. His fists clenched at his sides, then he flared his fingers out, deliberately trying to push down his desperate need to punch someone for putting her through this. He had to stay tethered. He couldn't screw it up and hurt her chances of being cleared. The fools on the other side of the door might risk Zellendine and all the people she could help for their ridiculous law, but he would try to get them to stop. By lying his ass off.

Rullon stood by his side, for all the universe like he couldn't care less that he had to escort his still apprentice son to this mess and that Troylus didn't hold secrets that could screw it all up.

Maybe Rullon had faith in his ability to do this, but Troylus's gut was down in his knees and telling him he sure didn't have faith in himself.

"You're angry," Rullon said, his voice barely audible.

"Of course," Troylus said, instead of the hell yes he wanted to say.

"There is only one option for you, then. Use it. If you let it take over, you'll screw this up. If you use it to help you focus on what you have to do and any pitfalls they leave open for you to fall into, then you'll do fine." Rullon put his hand out and turned his head toward the door to the meeting room, stopping the words in Troylus's mouth from coming.

A few seconds later, the door opened on Grandpa Kason's wizened face.

Somehow it seemed like Rullon knew he was coming, but Troylus didn't hear the old man's footsteps. Maybe the blood rushing through his head was just too damn loud.

"Rullon, Troylus, please come with me," Grandpa Kason said, a perfunctory smile on his face before he turned and left the door to fall closed, Troylus catching it before it shut completely.

He turned to his dad and raised an eyebrow before he followed, ushering Rullon in ahead of him.

The number of people gathered in the meeting room put his teeth on edge, he wasn't used to being around so many people at once, least of all when every single one of them turned to watch him as he walked to a chair on the dais.

But he had no choice other than to look at the people, every cell in his body wanted to look at Zellendine, but if he did they would probably count it against him. Even if they didn't, the likelihood he would give himself away by the look on his face was high.

No matter how hard he tried to keep his gaze away from her, as he took his seat and Alara cleared her throat, he made eye contact with Zellendine. To everyone else there she probably looked like nothing more than someone not nervous enough for the weight of what was happening. But he saw the set of her jaw, the perfectly straight posture and that not even her hands moved in her lap. She was so still, he might have thought she wasn't real except her chest rose and fell with each breath and he saw the hitch in her breathing when their eyes connected. He also saw that she was holding herself in check by sheer force of will and was still about to turn into a black hole and fold in on herself.

Damn it.

If Rullon wanted him to be mad, he should have told him to look at her like this. The blood pounding in his ears grew louder and faster, he curled his hands into fists and made no secret of how far out of orbit his thoughts were.

Alara stood up straighter and raised a brow when she looked at him and he turned his wrath filled face to her.

"Troylus, thank you for coming in here today and speaking with us." Her voice was honeyed and smooth and gave no indication like her face did that she even noticed his rage.

"When leadership calls," he said, his tone acerbic enough that both Zellendine and Rullon winced, but his words couldn't be indicted, and he knew it. By the tiniest narrowing of Grandpa Kason's eyes, it was clear he knew it too.

"Unfortunately, we're here because Zellendine is charged with looking back. Since you know her so well, we hoped you would be able to give us some insight into whether that were true or not." Grandpa Kason said, leaving his question unasked.

He let the silence grow, knowing better than to offer an explanation or bury himself with words unnecessarily. He got in trouble too much as a kid not to know better than to fall for petty tricks.

"You have been working with Zellendine to wake the sleepers, is that right?" Alara asked.

"I suppose," he said. "Working with is doing some heavy lifting there, though. She is doing all the work, and I'm just there to make sure she remembers to eat and to help with turning them to avoid bed sores."

The people gathered to watch shifted in their seats and averted their eyes.

Good, Troylus thought, being reminded that what she was doing was trying to help real people was uncomfortable when they were contemplating punishing her.

"Do you know anything about how she was going about waking them?" Grandpa Kason asked, pacing back and forth.

"She has some thing, like a small holo with all kinds of wires that end in sticky bits she puts on them to monitor their weird sleep pattern more closely, and then she was going to track herself and Briar and her dad." Troylus leaned forward, bracing his elbows on his knees.

"Now, why didn't she ask you to be a test for that?" Grandpa Kason stopped pacing to turn and face him.

"She did. But I don't really want her rooting around in my brain, so I haven't decided yet." Total lie, but it could have been true and that's all Troylus needed it to be.

"You and Zellendine have been friends for years, why have you been so upset with her this shift?" Alara asked, getting right to the point.

"Oh, I get it. That's why you want to talk to me, because you think I would be more likely to say something negative about her. Well, there's plenty to say, but I don't think any of it will mean much to you." He let them wait, to stand there and wonder if they should ask again, but he had a point and he wanted to make it and get everyone out of there, especially Zellendine.

"Listen, she is the perfect daughter of the Wheel, which probably seems like a great thing, but when I was disappointed that I was assigned to be a starwalker and not a medic while she got the medic position, she didn't understand. That sucked." Out of the corner of his eye, he was aware of Zellendine biting her lip and looking down at her hands before she recovered again.

Keep it up, Zellendine, he wanted to say. He wanted to find a way to give her encouragement, to tell her he was with her, would do anything for her, he loved her. But he couldn't, and he wasn't sure if he was ever going to get the chance. After he played the part of the person who loved her least, how would he ever be able to be her partner and convince her he would be better than Briar for her?

"Okay, so why were you both in the starwalker office late at night one night?" Grandpa Kason asked, a smile tugging at one corner of his mouth.

"She always wanted to go on a starwalk, and I thought if I could show her how boring most of the job was, I could get her to understand why I wanted something else. She didn't under-stand, but maybe that was because we have been anything but boring there lately. I really don't understand why you're all doing this. Zellendine would never do anything that wasn't right. Even I have to admit that," he said.

Alara glanced into the people watching, making eye contact with one of them.

Yanna was almost vibrating in her rage, and Troylus knew he was about to make it so much worse, but he had to make this stop.

I'm sorry, Yanna; you've been through too much, but I can't let Zellendine keep hurting, he said silently to her in his mind and then sat back in his chair, like the whole thing was beneath him.

"She even had me look at the computer system on the wombs because I know computers better than she does and she wanted to make sure she didn't miss anything that could explain what happened to that poor baby. Even though she knew it was a long shot, and she was supposed to be moving on to the sleepers completely, she couldn't let it go because she didn't have the answers." Troylus sat up and clenched his jaw, pushing his balled up fists into the seat beside his legs as Anders, choking back sobs, lurched from his seat and ran from the room. Yanna stayed in her seat, her normally pale skin turning red with a purple tinge.

Whatever using anger as a fuel meant to Rullon, the master was Yanna. Troylus was at a loss to understand how she remained upright, let alone ready to fight.

"My friends," Alara said, smiling at the people and moving to stand behind Zellendine's seat, "as much as I am sorry that so many tragedies have befallen us this shift, I think it is clear that this crew member did nothing wrong and that it is likely we are all just too saddened by what has transpired and are looking for someone to blame."

She put a hand on Zellendine's shoulder, who froze, barely breathing as she did. It was a major break of decorum, but Troylus wasn't worried about that and he suspected neither was Zellendine. He could tell Alara was about to clear her, but her hand so near Zellendine's neck made him want to grab Zellendine and run.

"I am sorry, Zellendine. You are cleared of these charges, and I hope you continue in your dogged pursuit to help the sleepers," Alara said while Grandpa Kason frowned and most of the watching people smiled.

Troylus stalked out of the meeting room, the people making way for him to pass, and he wondered if he still looked like he was using the anger that was coursing through his veins. Because it wasn't gone. At least not where the leadership was concerned. No, that rage was still very present in him.

53

ZELLENDINE

Part of her still couldn't believe it worked. Of all people to get the leadership to do what they wanted, Troylus did.

She looked past the milling crowd of people, hoping he would come back in to see her, but instead found the narrowed eyes of Grandpa Kason, standing off to the side and speaking with a barely controlled Yanna who looked anywhere but at Zellendine.

"Hey," Briar said, coming to her side and taking her hand. He smiled at her and leaned in to kiss her, she offered her cheek.

Maybe he would take it personally that she didn't want him to kiss her, but she hoped he would chalk it up to being in the meeting room and surrounded by leadership.

"There is no way you would look back, you won't even break decorum too much right now." Briar's smile was giant, like she was supposed to think it was a good thing he believed her to be so attached to the rules.

"Of course," she mumbled, while dreams of escaping the meeting room and finding Troylus to thank him filled her head.

He was possibly the only person in her life that actually knew her.

"Since we're low on time until you go into stasis, we should do something tonight, to celebrate," Briar said and her mouth dropped open.

Was he kidding? He had to be kidding. But, no. He looked for all the universe to be hopeful she would say yes.

"Zellendine has been locked up here for days now, I think it would be prudent for her to come back to our quarters and get a good meal and some rest before she does much of anything else," Stephen said, coming to her side.

She wasn't sure where he had been hiding in the throng, but she smiled at him and thanked the stars he showed when he did. And that he didn't want her to go with Briar.

"It really wasn't very comfortable to be in a closet for days other than to use a wet room. To even sleep sitting up in a closet, leaning against a wall," she said and smiled as they grimaced.

"I still can't believe they would think for a second you looked anywhere but forward," Briar said, shaking his head and squeezing her hand.

"Yeah," she mumbled, not paying attention because Yanna's conversation with Grandpa Kason was getting more animated.

"No," Yanna yelled, throwing her hands up.

The conversations all around quieted while everyone turned to look and the silence became another witness itself.

"Shh, please, Yanna," Grandpa Kason said, patting the air beside her shoulder like he couldn't quite manage to make himself touch her even though it was clearly needed to console her.

"I will not be quiet. Not now. My baby is dead and I'm the only person left who can speak up for him. I want answers. She didn't look. Not for real. Or she would be able to tell me something. I need to know." Yanna turned to Zellendine and lurched toward her, her face going from blotchy to ashen.

"Please. You have to know why. Please, just tell me why. Is it from me? Is it my fault? I need to know. My baby, I need to know for my baby." Yanna wailed, her shoulders collapsing while her chest heaved in sobs.

"Yanna, I'm so sorry. I wish your baby was with us too. I swear I do." Zellendine couldn't say more. She couldn't give Yanna what she needed even though she had it. She had to hide the answer until she could tell everyone so it wouldn't happen again. That was her new version of looking forward and she had to stay true to it. If she thought she could tell Yanna and be sure she could still stop it from happening to anyone else...

She reached a hand out toward Yanna and opened her mouth to ask her to talk to her later, in private, away from all these people.

But Yanna recoiled so much she fell into someone behind her.

"Don't touch me. You'll kill me just like you killed my baby." Yanna's voice was weak and wavering but her body was strong as she recovered from her stumble and stood up straight again.

"Please, Yanna, I didn't," Zellendine said, pulling her hand back, curling her fingers in, and holding it against her chest.

"You did." Yanna whipped her head from side to side, scanning the crowd, her eyes darting and her teeth bared. "You all did." She turned and ran, shoving people out of her way until she disappeared through the door.

54

TROYLUS

THE BARK OF THE TREE WAS ROUGH AGAINST THE BACK OF HIS head, and more noticeable than the last time he leaned against a tree in the orchard. His freshly cut hair was mostly Rullon's fault. Part of him wanted to go into the meeting room and face leadership with his hair out of regulation, but Rullon said it wouldn't help him to save Zellendine.

Maybe the old man was right, because it worked, didn't it? Then why did he feel like she wasn't saved at all?

His mind wandered, spinning faster than the ship, and still he couldn't make sense of it. Not his feelings for her, or her situation with Briar, and definitely not any of the strange things and terrible revelations of that shift.

"It just doesn't make any damn sense," he said aloud to no one but the dirt in his hand that he chucked away from him.

"Pretty sure talking to yourself is something you should see a medic about," Indigo said, rounding one of the trees in front of him with a smile and moving to sit next to him.

"Yeah, but a medic is the problem," Troylus said, dropping his head back to rest against the tree again.

She pulled her knees up and rested her arms across them, turning her head so she was looking his way, her lips pursed to the side and her eyes squinted at him.

"Oh," she said, sitting up and looking ahead into the trees. "Does Zellendine know?"

"No." He took a second though, to wonder if that were true. Did she know? He wasn't sure. "I mean, I don't think so."

"Well, you talked to leadership for her, if she knows you at all she knows how big that is. Maybe she does know." Indigo dropped her knees to the side and crisscrossed her legs, looking more at ease in the dirt and among the leaves than he thought he ever would anywhere.

"Maybe, but will it matter?" He didn't expect an answer, but had to smile when she offered one anyway.

"Sure. Why wouldn't it?" She looked at him, her eyebrows high.

"Because she is still with Briar." Troylus ran a hand through his hair, missing the rest of it when the gesture made his hand feel like it was missing half the length.

"Does she love him?" Indigo asked, getting straight to the important part like usual and irritating her brother in the process like usual too.

"Probably, although I can't figure out how when he doesn't know her at all." He shook his head, enjoying for a minute the near pain the movement induced on the back of his head. It was something to focus on that wasn't the gnawing sensation in his chest.

"What do you mean, doesn't know her?" Indigo turned her perceptive gaze on him and he knew he was treading in dangerous space.

Rullon accepted his looking back, and Zellendine's. But the odds of his sister being able to do the same when it was so much a part of their world, and she was so happy in it, with the assignment she got, and the partner she found, were slim.

"Just that I know her better now, after this shift, and I can say with one hundred percent accuracy that she isn't the girl I thought she was." And Briar still believed in that version of her.

"Briar probably knows that, don't you think?" Indigo looked up into the trees and seemed to be pushing away his concerns, which made him want to tell her all of it.

"She doesn't tell him some things because she thinks he'll take it wrong and it will cause problems." He bit his lip to stop himself from saying more.

"That's not good. Honesty with your partner is important. Even if you don't tell her how you feel, you should encourage her to be honest with Briar."

He stifled a laugh, if his sister only knew what she was asking him to say. Sure, Zellendine, tell Briar that you actually did break the law, was never going to come out of his mouth.

"Are you worried what will become of your friendship with Briar if you tell Zellendine how you feel?" she asked, turning toward him again.

"No. In fact I haven't thought about that much at all." He saw the disgust flash across her face. "I mean, of course I worry about that, but I've been a little occupied with other thoughts and this is only something I figured out today."

"Wait, really?" She put a hand on his arm and her eyebrows shot up.

"I don't know why you and Rullon seem so sure that I should have known, but trust me, I didn't." At the beginning of the shift he thought he hated her, not that it ever made sense, but he was so angry with her he couldn't even stand himself most of the time she was around.

"You are uniquely clueless then." She shook her head and

smiled at him, putting her hands in her lap and looking back at the trees.

"She snuck up on me. She was the most important thing in my world before I even knew she was aware of my universe."

"And she doesn't know." Indigo shook her head. "You should tell her exactly what you just told me." She bumped his shoulder with her own. "It was romantic."

He laughed and she laughed with him. For that second the ache in his chest was gone.

5 5

ZELLENDINE

Days of hiding in her quarters and sleeping as many hours as possible left her still sluggish as she walked down the hall toward the clinic and her first time working in too long. But with the next shift crew and her own shift's crew working the clinic they could afford to give her time to recover from almost having her future stolen.

But being out of her bed and headed to work made her hands want to shake. She was taken from the clinic. Maybe it would never be fully comfortable for her to be there again when every time she thought about it the first thing that popped into her head was the lack of oxygen that happened when they told her she had to go to speak with leadership and she knew.

If Troylus came to see her, though, maybe then she would feel comfortable again.

She told herself she knew why she was left alone for days by everyone other than her dad. She told herself Troylus was smart to stay away, it was his supposed distance from her that gave him the ability to get her out of trouble. She told herself she understood, and it was for the best. But she wanted to see him. She had not thought of Briar once.

As the curve of the hallway revealed more of the corridor in front of her and she lifted her eyes from the floor, she jumped.

Halfway down the hall, Yanna stood next to the chute panel her baby was sent to the stars from.

Instead of the ravaged woman she had been every time Zellendine saw her since her baby died, Yanna looked like a tragic work of art.

She stood in the hall, her hands holding a small blanket close to her chest, her hair wasn't pulled back or greasy, it flowed down her shoulders, free and loose. She was in a nightgown, something that must have been passed down to her as it wasn't regulation at all, and it was soft ivory with tiny flowers and lace at the bottom and the capped sleeves. But the most changed thing about her was her face.

Gone were the splotchy red patches and the purple rage. Instead her skin was as pale as her nightgown and the only color to it was deep blue bruise-like circles under her eyes. Eyes that cried a torrent of tears.

"Yanna," Zellendine said, her voice like an exhalation, but Yanna looked up and made eye contact, a smile blooming on her face.

Zellendine took a careful step forward, and another, not looking way from the eyes of the woman in front of her.

"Are you okay? Do you need me to get Anders?" Zellendine asked.

The smile fell from her face and was replaced by a line between her brows and even more tears.

Zellendine wanted to scream for someone to come and talk to Yanna. Someone to help this woman who was clearly still struggling. But she didn't want to scare her so she just kept up her slow walk forward, picking each step with care, her footfalls so gradual the rickety old floor barely made a sound.

"Sometimes I dream of my baby crying," Yanna said, her voice scratchy and hushed.

Her brain yelled, say something, but Zellendine couldn't find the words.

"Did that really happen? Did my baby cry, even once?" Yanna asked, tilting her head at her and bringing the blanket in her hands to the side of her face.

What was okay to say? Anything? Whatever she said she needed to get Yanna better help than she was. That had to be her goal.

"I'm sorry, Yanna. But the baby was born deceased and never cried." Zellendine reached Yanna's side and wanted to touch her shoulder, lead her away from the sad place in the hall.

"Maybe it's a message. Maybe my baby is telling me to join him." Yanna smiled again, although tears never stopped running down her face to drip off her chin.

Zellendine's heart dropped to her knees and the hairs on her arms stood on end. She had to stop Yanna from hurting herself. She couldn't let her, but she didn't know what to do.

Tears pressed at the back of her eyes and she choked on the first attempt to speak.

"Perhaps it's a message that you'll have another baby." She tried for reassuring but Yanna recoiled from her.

"Not as a replacement at all, but as a way for your first baby to prepare you for a new one. A way for your first baby to make you forgive them for not staying because they didn't want to go, but they had to." Zellendine wasn't even sure what she was saying anymore. She was grasping at anything to make the situation not as broken, to save Yanna even though she couldn't save her baby.

Yanna's face crumpled and her shoulders folded in, she wilted to the ground, grasping at the handle to chute as she fell.

She clung to the cold metal handle and wept, wracking sobs that made the tears at the back of Zellendine's eyes tumble down her cheeks.

"Oh, Yanna. I'm so sorry this happened. I'm so, so sorry," she said, sitting next to her on the floor and throwing protocol away to reach out a hand and place a feather light touch on Yanna's shoulder.

"I'm sorry, baby." Yanna wailed.

Zellendine closed her eyes and tried to hold in her own cries; she had to let Yanna have her time. It wasn't fair to interrupt, but oh, universe, why did the Chapter have to be so wrong? Why did they have to do this to Yanna and all the others, why?

"My poor baby." Yanna's voice was smoothing out and Zellendine opened her eyes as Yanna continued to crumple, letting go of the handle and falling into herself, burying her face in the tiny blanket, her tears never even slowing.

The tears pouring down Zellendine's face never stopped, and she didn't take her hand off of Yanna's shoulder, leaving it there to offer the insignificant amount of support she could give.

"So, the crying I hear is proof that it's okay?" Yanna asked, looking up from the blanket and speaking around her hiccuping.

"Nothing is okay about your baby being gone, but I think it's a message that you can have another baby and it's okay to do that." Zellendine tried to pick her words carefully, the last thing she wanted was to make it all worse with a careless phrase.

"I'm… I'm pregnant," Yanna said. "I didn't think it was possible. It's not supposed to be possible while we're in deep space."

Zellendine coughed, choking on her surprise. Theoretically,

all those menstrual cycles stopped other than the initial menses during puberty for all the people onboard while they were in deep space. No one had ever gotten pregnant naturally while in space. But… the birds.

"The birds in the orchard are nesting again; maybe your body knows we're close to our planet just like theirs do," Zellendine said, venturing a small smile that Yanna returned while her hands went to her stomach.

TROYLUS

"ZELLENDINE'S BACK AT THE CLINIC TODAY," PARMITA SAID AS HE took off his helmet and she helped him with the rest of his walking suit.

"I heard. Not sure how she keeps at it when she got shit on so bad, but good for her. I hope she can figure out how to wake the sleepers, we're almost out of time," he said, pulling his arms out. It didn't matter that Rullon told him before Parmita did, every time he heard her name a chill went through his body.

"Well, aren't you going to go check on her, you're her hero after all." Parmita gave him a wry grin and a raised brow.

"Very funny." He didn't want to let her know how much he didn't want to go see Zellendine. Every single part of him wanted to see her, talk to her, hold her, but he didn't want to do it until she got rid of Briar on her own without his influencing her decision at all, and that meant not seeing her. Besides, he wasn't sure she would even welcome what he wanted to tell her, and that made his heart race worse than any spacewalk ever had.

"Come on, Troylus. Don't be a killjoy," Parmita said,

bumping him so he toppled over into the wall with one leg out of his suit.

"Remind me to get you back for that one," he said, shaking his head and smiling as she winked at him.

"Only if you go to Zellendine because you are a miserable ass when you're keeping yourself from her." Parmita took the last piece of his suit and put it away while his mouth opened and closed on a smart retort that he never managed to figure out.

"Fine, just so I get to shove you around next time," he said, flashing her a grin as she stuck her tongue out and he turned on his heel to head to the cryo bay. If he knew Zellendine the way he thought he did, she was going to go straight from her first day back at the clinic to her first day in the cryo bay helping the people still trapped in their dreams.

Passing the clinic, he was surprised by the number of people just loitering around the entryway. Weird.

They were talking in hushed tones and kept sneaking glances through the doorway but looking in himself didn't show him anything. There weren't even any people in the front area of the clinic. Whatever the people outside were looking for, he didn't think they were going to find it by standing around in the hall.

By the time the door to the cryo bay came into view he was adjusting his uniform and running a hand through his hair, hoping he didn't look like a giant mess. What was he going to say? What in the universe would she say back?

He could barely think and the blood was rushing through his head again by the time he walked through the door.

The room was silent other than a steady if rapid tapping. The sleepers were still in their tanks, the families no longer visiting every single day as they grew too busy with their duties and their lives on board. Some of them were trying hard to forget just so they could move forward. It never ceased to piss him off that so many people thought following their stupid rule was more important than looking back to check on their loved ones.

He rounded the corner and there, between the rows of tanks, was Zellendine.

She sat in her chair, tapping away at her holo at speeds that made it hard for him to even follow her fingers. She stared down at what she was doing with her mouth twisted to the side and zero idea he was even there. A piece of her long blonde hair had escaped her plait and hung down along her cheekbone.

Troylus moved to her side, crouching down next to her and staring at her dark brown eyes that still didn't see him but that he saw everything in.

Reaching out a hand that only had a slight tremble, he tucked the piece of hair behind her ear.

Zellendine snapped her head up and her whole face softened when she saw it was him, her mouth turning up in a smile that melted the hard knot in his stomach.

Her arms wrapped around him, the holo pressing against his back and he hugged her close, burying his face in her neck.

"You didn't come to the clinic," she said, her voice muffled against him sounded like she was smiling.

"No, there was too much to say and you were supposed to be working," he said, but his smile was brittle.

They pulled apart enough for her to put her head against his chest with a sigh.

"On my way here, I passed the clinic and something is going on over there, I thought maybe you were still there coming up with a way to wake everyone up." He leaned his cheek against the top of her head.

She sat up, her eyes wide and tears were forming at the corners.

"Zellendine," he said, putting a hand on her cheek, "what happened?"

"Yanna, she... I think she was trying to commit suicide."

Troylus sucked in a breath and squeezed his eyes shut, not wanting to let himself imagine the depth of the pain she must have been in, but not being able to stop it.

"But she forgave me. And, I think she'll be able to get some help now." Zellendine took a shuddering breath and Troylus wiped a thumb along her cheekbone to clear away the one tear that was glistening there.

"At some point you're going to have to tell me how you never got pissed with her and always just accepted that she blamed you."

"Probably," she said, smiling at him and her eyes softening, "the same way you manage to keep saving my ass when I don't say thank you often enough."

"Well, the first time didn't really count. It was an accident." He smiled at her and she laughed.

"So, I shouldn't say thank you for that one, got it. What about this time, then? Should I tell you that every moment I spend on the planet is going to be because of you?"

"That's different," he said, his heart pounding and his mind screaming at him to tell her, that this was the time.

"You do good things for me because you're a good person. I don't take it personally that Yanna was mad at me because, hopefully, I'm a good person too. How is that different?" she asked, the smile still on her face.

"Because..." He couldn't say it. The words were bright and loud in his head, but he couldn't get them out of his mouth and past his suddenly parched throat.

Instead, he leaned in and paused. She didn't move away. He leaned in a closed his eyes as their lips met.

Something in him gave way, an explosion in his chest, it

flooded out of him in waves. Not down his limbs, but from the center of him it flowed.

Zellendine pulled back, her eyes wide and her mouth open in awe. She was tinted blue, everything was through Troylus's vision. All he could see was blue.

57

ZELLENDINE

"Troylus," she said, catching him as he slouched over, the blue light no longer pouring out of him. "Are... are you okay?"

He blinked, slow, his eyes unfocused.

"Please, Troylus, I need you to talk to me. Tell me you're okay, please." He started to right himself, to sit up and shake his head, blinking until he focused on her face with a squint.

"Zellendine? I... did it happen again? It did, didn't it?" he asked, his voice hoarse and more exhausted than she had ever heard it before.

She dropped her head and sucked down a deep breath, "You're okay. You're going to be okay." She wrapped him up in her arms and squeezed him tight to her chest.

"But did that just happen?" He buried his face in her neck, but his hold on her back was weaker than it had been.

"Yes," she said, pulling back and looking him up and down to check for any damage.

"I'm sorry." He closed his eyes and she wanted to kiss him again, to make him understand that she wasn't.

Moving forward, she stopped, because a cough sounded

from Upton's tank. Her heart sank as she turned, expecting to see someone on the other side of the stack, watching them.

But it wasn't someone who just walked in.

It was Upton, dragging his hand up to his eyes to rub at them.

"Oh, universe," she yelled, jumping to the side of his tank. "Upton, buddy, can you hear me?"

"Zell… Zellendine?" he asked, voice raw and barely there.

"I'll go get Stephen," Troylus said, standing up behind her and catching himself on the stack.

"No. Troylus, you stay here. You might fall over." She stood and sat him on her chair, kissing his cheek and giving him a smile before she darted from the room.

Down the corridor she sprinted, dodging the few people she saw, until she got close to the clinic and saw the gathering of people and she slowed up.

She still darted through the gathering of people at a speed beyond what was polite, leaving at least one person grumbling in her wake. Not that she cared. Her blood was buzzing and her heart was flying as she went through the doorway into the observation office her dad was in while he watched over a sleeping Yanna.

He looked up at her and started to stand before the words were out of her mouth.

"Upton's awake," she said, her pitch high and thready.

Zellendine sucked down a breath and Stephen jumped to the office next door, bursting in as Dean was stitching someone up.

"I have to go to cryo," Stephen said.

"Go, I'll watch her." Dean gestured with his head for them to leave, his smile wide.

They went back out of the clinic and down the hallway at only a fraction slower the pace she left the cryo bay at.

By the time they got to where Troylus still sat in the chair next to the stack, she was out of breath and left it up to her dad to look in the tanks above and see that all of the occupants were awake.

She leaned against the stack next to the sleepers and took deep breaths until Troylus came to her side and put a hand on hers. She bit her lip and looked into his dear eyes.

Not once in the years she was with Briar and immune to even noticing any one else as someone she would ever want to kiss had she wanted to kiss him as much as she wanted to kiss Troylus at that moment. He looked so scared, his gaze kept returning to her dad and the tanks full of people he saved with his world remaking power.

But she was more scared to do what she wanted than she had ever been. She bit her lip and swallowed, hard, knowing that if she did, she risked his ability springing to life. And she had no idea what it would do the next time that happened.

They stood silent and watched as Stephen did the checks, helping the sleepers understand what was happening, what they went through.

Eventually, people arrived, the families of the sleeping, notified by someone she passed in her mad dash, or maybe even by Dean. It didn't matter how they knew, they did, and they came.

Journo and Briar appeared beside her, Briar pulling her into a rough hug while he cried and said, "thank you," again and again.

She floated in her mind through it all, disconnected from the moment, her supposed triumph, by the truth.

"How did this happen?" Grandpa Kason asked her dad.

"They all show evidence of a low grade shock right before coming out of REM, but you'll have to ask Zellendine. She woke them while I was in the clinic," Stephen said.

Grandpa Kason turned to look her way.

Briar had his arms around her, but her eyes sought out Troylus.

Troylus furrowed his brow and thinned his lips before he turned to Grandpa Kason and squared his shoulders.

"I stopped by to see how she was doing and Zellendine used some trick in her equipment to give them a shock; she said it was the only thing left to try," Troylus said and she tried to breathe around the lump lodged in her throat.

Every set of eyes in the room focused on her, the lie Troylus told them shining in each.

"There is a tool we use when we need to stimulate a heart." She didn't bother explaining that it was only used when a heart was stopped, she didn't think that would help the narrowing of Grandpa Kason's eyes.

But the other people in the room looked at her with reverence she didn't deserve, and Troylus looked at her with sadness.

She watched in silence as Troylus left the cryo bay, knowing she was going to need to pretend that not only was she the one who saved the sleepers, but that she didn't love the one who did. And it didn't matter how she felt. Because acting on her feelings risked everything.

58

TROYLUS

It took everything in him not to run to Zellendine. Not to push Briar aside from where he was loitering behind her, seemingly unaware of the panic taking over her body, and run to her, tell her everything would be alright, that he would make sure she woke up.

After everything they had been through, he was sure he could wake her up. Even if it were to happen again, he could wake everyone up. At least he knew that now. He didn't know if she would want his help, she certainly didn't want his love.

But she stood, staring at the tank she was supposed to climb into and he could see from his place across the room that her chest was heaving, sucking in giant gulps of breath, her hands were in white-knuckled fists clenched at her sides, and she wasn't thinking about him freeing the sleepers, she was thinking about there being sleepers at all.

More than he had ever wanted anything, he wanted to go to her and hold her until she was calm, until she was able to do this, to keep up the façade, the lie they had sold. Not just for her, but for all the rest of the shift's people who were climbing into their own tanks, trusting that they had solved the problem.

What they had actually done was accidentally fixed the problem. Although he had freed all the sleepers of the tanks, he wasn't entirely sure it wouldn't repeat because he wasn't certain what he had done, what switch he had flipped. All they could do was hope the rest of the shifts had no problems and he could wake them all if they did once they were coming out of stasis for their final approach to the planet.

Rullon walked up to him, yawning.

"Are you actually tired?" Troylus asked, his voice a little too loud in the hope Zellendine would hear him and look his way so he could give her a reassuring smile or something.

"Yes, I know it doesn't make any sense, but every time we go into stasis, I am exhausted. It's like my body just sees the tanks and says, okay, perfect time to sleep. But that isn't even what we're doing. Not really. I don't know, it doesn't make any sense." Rullon laughed at himself and stretched.

It didn't make any sense, but it did roil Troylus's stomach. Just his father mentioning sleeping made his throat dry.

Troylus gave his father a low laugh in return and rubbed a hand over his face, looking again toward Zellendine and wishing she had been right. If she had, maybe this day wouldn't make her shoulders curl, and wouldn't make him want to break protocol, something they couldn't afford, to make her feel better.

All he could do was wait until she saw him, all he could do was stand there and hope she looked his way. All he could do was try to offer her the face of surety from the one person who actually knew what was going on. He hoped it would be enough.

59

ZELLENDINE

It didn't matter that the sleepers were awake, it didn't matter that she was supposedly cleared of the charges against her, looking at the cryo tank she was supposed to be in for the next one hundred years made her hands shake and sweat break out in the small of her back.

She looked across the room and made eye contact with Troylus, he nodded her way and a tremulous smile played on his face, like he was trying to reassure her.

Fat chance of that. She appreciated the gesture though, so she tried to smile back at him.

He turned to climb into his own tank while people milled around the room, hugging their loved ones and doing what Troylus was, climbing in. She wanted to run to him, to kiss him, apologize, and thank him, but all she could do was watch from across the room as he still tried to help her.

Zellendine looked back at her tank and swallowed, hard. A need to drink a million glasses of water built inside her. She used to get in and go to sleep without a second thought, without a single concern. Just like she did when she went to sleep in her quarters. Now… now she folded her fingers into fists at her sides, trying to stop the shaking, but it moved up her arms.

She crossed her arms in front of her and looked back toward Troylus in his tank. He was sitting up, his knees bent in front of him with his arms across the top of them, and staring at her, his face showing concern, but only for her. He didn't seem to have a single care for himself. Or Rullon, who patted him on the shoulder and climbed into the bunk between him and Zellendine.

Troylus flashed a smile at his dad and looked back at her again, nodding once, his mouth turning up at the corners in a subdued smile.

"See you in the morning," Stephen said, making her jump as he set his hand on her shoulder and made his way past her to his own tank.

Every time they went into stasis, he said it, but this time the last thing she wanted to do was laugh or say it back.

"Yeah," she said, her voice sounding like a scratch of a chair across a floor to her own ears. Her father didn't seem to notice, just continuing on to his tank and climbing in.

He believed her. He must have believed her lie that they knew why the sleepers had been unable to wake up, he must have thought there was nothing to worry about.

"Zellendine," Troylus said, his voice right behind her, low and soft.

She wasn't sure when he climbed back out of his tank, but she was just glad he had, that he was there. She turned and fought the urge to put her head against his chest. The other people getting into their tanks around them wouldn't under-stand why she was so afraid, only Troylus knew.

"What if?" she asked under her breath. She couldn't say the rest of her question out loud, but she didn't need to, Troylus closed his eyes for a second and took a deep breath before he touched her hand, fleetingly, with his own.

"No matter what, I will make it okay," he said.

Her breathing hitched as she tried to fill her lungs, slow and long, to force her heart to calm. He was right. Whatever happened, he was going to be able to make it okay, he did it before.

"Okay?" he asked.

She bit her lip and nodded, repeating his voice in her head saying okay over and over.

"Troy, Zelle, I'm glad you guys aren't asleep yet. Sorry I had to step away for a second," Briar said, coming to stand next to both of them with a smile on his face.

"You barely made it back to her in time." Troylus stepped back from Zellendine, making way for Briar. She wanted to snatch him back. "I'll see you both when we wake up and then we won't have to do this again," Troylus said, flashing them a grin and heading back to his tank.

Zellendine watched him go, focusing so hard on the promise that this would be their last stasis, she was barely aware of Briar putting his hand on the small of her back and leaning into her, until his lips were on hers.

She closed her eyes and pretended to kiss him back, but she pulled away and turned toward her tank when he tried to deepen the kiss.

He followed her as she climbed in, unaware that her heart hammered an uneven rhythm in her chest.

"I can't wait until everyone is awake and we get to spend more than a month together," Briar said, a big grin on his face as he crouched down beside her tank.

On the other side of Rullon's tank she watched as Troylus climbed into his. He looked at her one more time and gave her a soft smile and a nod before he laid back.

"Yeah," she said, looking back at Briar and allowing herself to wonder what it would be like to have her feet on the ground of the new planet. She wondered what it would be like to meet the rest of the population of the ship, to spend more than a month trying to love Briar, to spend more time with Troylus. Then she forced herself to stop down that road, it was full of more complications she wasn't prepared to deal with.

"When you wake up, I'll be waking up too. It's been so long since that happened, I'm not sure what it will be like not to have you there when I open my eyes." He leaned in to kiss her and she turned her face so that they kissed each other's cheeks, wrapping her arms around his neck.

It didn't feel right to kiss him anymore, she was keeping things from him, lying to him, she didn't feel the same about him. Every time he touched her it only reminded her that she wasn't who he thought she was. He still thought she was innocent of the charges, but she was actually just cleared, and no matter how much she wanted to tell him the truth, his reaction to the charges told her she couldn't. Every time he touched her it reminded her that she wanted the person who really knew and accepted her to be the one touching her, and she couldn't have that.

The only person she felt like she could trust was Troylus, but he was going into stasis, and it wasn't Briar's fault. So, she held onto Briar's neck and fought the tears pressing at the back of her eyes.

Maybe when they woke up and got to the planet things would be better, maybe by the time they landed she and Troylus would understand the blue light, maybe then she could forgive herself for keeping Briar in the dark. And maybe she would know what to do.

Briar relaxed against her and kissed her hair before he

unwound his arms and pulled back from her with a sweet smile on his face.

She nodded to him and laid back in her tank, sweat breaking out along her hairline and her throat back to dry. Her hand shook, making it hard for her to even meet her target as she reached out and pushed the button to close the tank.

Through the glass window of the tank she watched Briar lean over and mouth 'I love you, see you in the morning' like he always did, his hand on the glass over her heart. She smiled back at him and before she could mouth see you in the morning back to him like always, she watched as a shine of silver grew in the corner of his eye.

Her mind screamed that it couldn't be happening again, that Briar's eyes couldn't be changing like Troylus's had. But as she watched and her own eyelids grew heavy, her hand no longer listening to her plea to reach out toward him, the flash of silver turned into a sliver, a slice of shining metallic color taking over the blue grey of his iris, growing into a section large enough she could no longer deny it. Briar's eyes were changing.

AFTERWORD

Thank you for reading!

The next book in the series, The Spindle, is now available.

If you enjoyed this book, please leave a review at your favorite vendor.

If you would like to be the first to hear about the next book in the series, and get a free book, please head on over to jdarleneeverly.com and sign up for the newsletter.

ACKNOWLEDGMENTS

A whole hearted thank you to my family and friends. A big bag of thanks to Jupiter Alley, Magnolia Editing, and the team at Wishing Well. Sometimes the characters don't leave you alone, and they're usually right.